# *Relationships*—

friend to friend, father to daughter, white to black, young
to old—are at the core of these nine stories by Robert
Cormier. Revealing introductions, written especially for
each story, tell as much about the author and his craft as
they do about the unforgettable characters in the stories
themselves.

The stories probe the feelings and reactions of people in
life's most trying situations: a first love, leaving for college, a
boy's discovery that his father is all too human.

Here is a glimpse of Robert Cormier from a different
angle—warm, touching, and intensely personal.

# EIGHT *plus* ONE

STORIES *by* ROBERT CORMIER

PANTHEON BOOKS

ACKNOWLEDGMENTS

"The Moustache," "A Bad Time for Fathers," and
"Mine on Thursdays" were originally published in
*Woman's Day*.
"President Cleveland, Where Are You?" and "Bunny Berigan—
Wasn't He a Musician or Something?" were originally
published in *Redbook*.
"Another of Mike's Girls" was originally published
in *McCalls Magazine*.
"My First Negro" was originally published in *Sign*.
"Protestants Cry, Too" was originally published
in *St. Anthony Messenger*.
"Guess What? I Almost Kissed My Father Goodnight"
was originally published in *The Saturday Evening Post*.

*Published in the United States by Pantheon Books,
a division of Random House, Inc., New York,
and simultaneously in Canada by Random House
of Canada Limited, Toronto.
Library of Congress Cataloging in Publication Data
Cormier, Robert. 8 plus 1.
Contents: The Moustache.—Mine on Thursdays. —
Another of Mike's girls. [etc.]
[1. Family life—Fiction. 2. Short stories] I. Title.
PZ7.C81634 Ei [Fic] 80-13512
ISBN 0-394-84595-1 ISBN 0-394-94595-6 (lib. bdg.)
Manufactured in the United States of America
1 2 3 4 5 6 7 8 9 10*

*To My Brothers and Sisters,*
*John and Charles*
*Gloria, Ann, and Connie*
*And to the Memory of Norman and Leo*

# A Note by the Author

$T$he stories in this collection were written between 1965 and 1975. They were written at a time when my wife and I were involved in bringing up three teenagers. The house sang those days with the vibrant songs of youth—tender, hectic, tragic, and ecstatic. Hearts were broken on Sunday afternoon and repaired by the following Thursday evening, but how desperate it all was in the interim. The telephone never stopped ringing, the shower seemed to be constantly running, the Beatles became a presence in our lives.

As our son and two daughters went through those lacerating adolescent years, I recalled my own teenage era and realized that my children were reenacting my own life and the lives of friends I had known. It struck me that fashions change along with slang and pop tunes and fads, but emotions remain the same. A bruised heart is a bruised heart no matter what year it is.

My memory may falter when it comes to facts and figures, but I have almost total recall of my emotions at almost any given moment of the past. Thus, I began to write a series of short stories, translating the emotions of both the present and the past—and finding they were the same, actually— into stories dealing with family relationships, fathers and mothers, daughters and sons. I wrote about growing up, and the parents in the stories grow up, too, to the knowledge, often bittersweet, that the passing years bring.

*Three stories deal with the days of the Great Depression or immediately afterward while the remainder are set in scenes contemporary with the time in which they were written. I didn't edit the stories or alter them. It is my hope that the emotions ring true; if they do, then I have done my work properly.*

*A few years ago, I spoke at a seminar at Simmons College in Boston, one of my favorite stopping places for seminars. A woman approached me timidly after I had talked to the participants. She said that she had almost not attended my particular segment of the program because she had recently read my novels* The Chocolate War *and* I Am the Cheese *and feared she would encounter a monster. She told me that she was glad she came, however, because she had met "another Robert Cormier."*

*I hope readers of my novels will meet that other Robert Cormier in these stories.*

# Contents

A Note by the Author    vii

The Moustache    1

Mine on Thursdays    17

Another of Mike's Girls    39

President Cleveland, Where Are You?    57

A Bad Time for Fathers    75

Protestants Cry, Too    93

Guess What? I Almost Kissed
My Father Goodnight    115

My First Negro    135

Bunny Berigan—Wasn't He a Musician
or Something?    155

# The Moustache 🌱

# Introduction ✌

*T*he question I hear most often when the subject of writing comes up is "Where do you get your ideas?" No doubt that's the question all writers hear most frequently.

Every writer has his or her own answer, of course. I tell people that my ideas usually grow out of an emotion— something I have experienced, observed, or felt. The emotion sparks my impulse to write and I find myself at the typewriter trying to get the emotion and its impact down on paper. Out of that comes a character and then a plot. The sequence seldom varies: emotion, character, plot. Each element contributes to the whole.

Which brings up further questions. Where do the characters come from? Are they made up? And where do you get your plots?

Perhaps the best way to answer the questions is to explain the genesis of "The Moustache" because it follows almost perfectly the method I have applied throughout the years, showing how a strong emotion caused me to use real people and situations to produce a short story that is entirely fiction.

When my son, Peter, was a teenager, his maternal grandmother became a resident in a local nursing home. The victim of an accident from which she never really recovered —she was struck by a car as she crossed a street—she had more recently suffered the terrible onslaught of arteriosclerosis. Those were shattering days for us all, particularly my wife, who visited her daily but found little comfort because her mother often did not recognize her.

Her mother had been a handsome, vigorous woman, capable of operating a drugstore for many years following the early death of her husband. It was cruel to see her diminished as a person. It was sad to have her grandchildren witness her deterioration from the "Mémère" they had known as youngsters.

One Saturday, Peter visited her in the nursing home. He returned visibly moved, shaken. Her condition had affected him greatly. His grandmother had been uncommunicative, ravaged by the disease, only a dim echo of the Mémère he had known and loved throughout his boyhood.

I remembered my own maternal grandmother, a lively, lovely woman who had died suddenly while I was in high school. I had been stunned by the way she had looked in her coffin. Her lips were two thin straight lines. She looked grim and forbidding, nothing at all like the vibrant Nana I had known. I left the funeral parlor in anguish. Those lips haunted me.

Now, almost thirty years later, Peter's emotion had merged with mine and I found myself struggling to express it at the typewriter.

What emerged was "The Moustache."

These were the realities: Peter's grandmother was in a nursing home. He had visited her. He was a teenager and had recently grown a moustache. His grandmother had had little recognition of him. He had been shaken by the visit.

Here is what happened in the story that grew out of these elements and emotions: A boy who had recently grown a moustache visits his grandmother in a nursing home. Because of the moustache, she mistakenly thinks he is someone else. As a result, the boy sees his grandmother as a person, not simply the grandmother figure he'd always known. The moment also caused him to grow a bit and to make him look at his world and his parents in a different way.

Thus, the stuff of actuality is transformed into the stuff of fiction.

The underlying problem, of course, is to have the characters appear as distinct personalities of their own and not carbon copies of the actual people. In effect, I have used real emotions but the people are real only on the printed page—the boy in the story is not Peter and the woman is not his grandmother.

One note: My wife's father, who died at an early age, was a man of magnificent gestures. In the heart of the Depression while he was struggling with a new business and bringing up a family, he bought his wife—my children's Mémère—a baby-grand piano. This marvelous gift in the bleakest of times has never failed to arouse my admiration for that man. The piano is now in our living room, and I have used the incident twice in short stories, one of them "The Moustache."

# The Moustache 🌱

At the last minute Annie couldn't go. She was invaded by one of those twenty-four-hour flu bugs that sent her to bed with a fever, moaning about the fact that she'd also have to break her date with Handsome Harry Arnold that night. We call him Handsome Harry because he's actually handsome, but he's also a nice guy, cool, and he doesn't treat me like Annie's kid brother, which I am, but like a regular person. Anyway, I had to go to Lawnrest alone that afternoon. But first of all I had to stand inspection. My mother lined me up against the wall. She stood there like a one-man firing squad, which is kind of funny because she's not like a man at all, she's very feminine, and we have this great relationship—I mean, I feel as if she really likes me. I realize that sounds strange, but I know guys whose mothers love them and cook special stuff for them and worry about them and all but there's something missing in their relationship.

Anyway. She frowned and started the routine.

"That hair," she said. Then admitted: "Well, at least you combed it."

I sighed. I have discovered that it's better to sigh than argue.

"And that moustache." She shook her head. "I still say a seventeen-year-old has no business wearing a moustache."

"It's an experiment," I said. "I just wanted to see if I

could grow one." To tell the truth, I had proved my point about being able to grow a decent moustache, but I also had learned to like it.

"It's costing you money, Mike," she said.

"I know, I know."

The money was a reference to the movies. The Downtown Cinema has a special Friday night offer—half-price admission for high school couples, seventeen or younger. But the woman in the box office took one look at my moustache and charged me full price. Even when I showed her my driver's license. She charged full admission for Cindy's ticket, too, which left me practically broke and unable to take Cindy out for a hamburger with the crowd afterward. That didn't help matters, because Cindy has been getting impatient recently about things like the fact that I don't own my own car and have to concentrate on my studies if I want to win that college scholarship, for instance. Cindy wasn't exactly crazy about the moustache, either.

Now it was my mother's turn to sigh.

"Look," I said, to cheer her up. "I'm thinking about shaving it off." Even though I wasn't. Another discovery: You can build a way of life on postponement.

"Your grandmother probably won't even recognize you," she said. And I saw the shadow fall across her face.

Let me tell you what the visit to Lawnrest was all about. My grandmother is seventy-three years old. She is a resident—which is supposed to be a better word than *patient*—at the Lawnrest Nursing Home. She used to make the greatest turkey dressing in the world and was a nut about baseball and could even quote batting averages, for crying out loud. She always rooted for the losers. She was in love with the Mets until they started to win. Now she has arteriosclerosis, which the dictionary says is "a chronic disease characterized by abnormal thickening and hardening of the arterial walls." Which really means that she can't live at home anymore or even with us, and her memory has betrayed her as well as her body. She used to wander off and sometimes didn't recognize people. My mother visits her all the time, driving the thirty miles to Lawnrest almost every day. Because Annie was home for a semester break from college, we had decided to make a special Saturday visit. Now Annie was in bed, groaning theatrically—she's a drama major—but I told my mother I'd go, anyway. I hadn't seen my grandmother since she'd been admitted to Lawnrest. Besides, the place is located on the Southwest Turnpike, which meant I could barrel along in my father's new Le Mans. My ambition was to see the speedometer hit seventy-five. Ordinarily, I used the old station wagon, which can barely stagger up to fifty.

Frankly, I wasn't too crazy about visiting a nursing home. They reminded me of hospitals and hospitals turn me off. I mean, the smell of ether makes me nauseous, and I feel faint at the sight of blood. And as I approached Lawnrest—which is a terrible cemetery kind of name, to begin with—I was sorry I hadn't avoided the trip. Then I felt guilty about it. I'm loaded with guilt complexes. Like driving like a madman after promising my father to be careful. Like sitting in the parking lot, looking at the nursing home with dread and thinking how I'd rather be with Cindy. Then I thought of all the Christmas and birthday gifts my grandmother had given me and I got out of the car, guilty, as usual.

Inside, I was surprised by the lack of hospital smell, although there was another odor or maybe the absence of an odor. The air was antiseptic, sterile. As if there was no atmosphere at all or I'd caught a cold suddenly and couldn't taste or smell.

A nurse at the reception desk gave me directions—my grandmother was in East Three. I made my way down the tiled corridor and was glad to see that the walls were painted with cheerful colors like yellow and pink. A wheelchair suddenly shot around a corner, self-propelled by an old man, white-haired and toothless, who cackled merrily as he barely missed me. I jumped aside—here I was, almost getting wiped out by a two-mile-an-hour wheelchair after doing seventy-five on the pike. As I walked through the corridor seeking East Three, I couldn't help glancing into the rooms, and it was like some kind of wax museum—all these figures in various stances and attitudes, sitting in beds or chairs, standing at windows, as if they were frozen forever in these postures. To tell the truth, I began to hurry because I was getting depressed. Finally, I saw a beautiful girl approaching, dressed in white, a nurse or an attendant, and I was so happy to see someone young, someone walking and acting normally, that I gave her a wide smile and a big hello and I must have looked like a kind of nut. Anyway, she looked right through me as if I were a window, which is about par for the course whenever I meet beautiful girls.

I finally found the room and saw my grandmother in bed. My grandmother looks like Ethel Barrymore. I never knew who Ethel Barrymore was until I saw a terrific movie, *None But the Lonely Heart*, on TV, starring Ethel Barrymore and Cary Grant. Both my grandmother and Ethel Barrymore have these great craggy faces like the side of a mountain and wonderful voices like syrup being poured. Slowly. She was propped up in bed, pillows puffed behind her. Her hair had been combed out and fell upon her shoulders. For some reason, this flowing hair gave her an almost girlish appearance, despite its whiteness.

She saw me and smiled. Her eyes lit up and her eyebrows arched and she reached out her hands to me in greeting. "Mike, Mike," she said. And I breathed a sigh of relief. This was one of her good days. My mother had warned me that she might not know who I was at first.

I took her hands in mine. They were fragile. I could actually feel her bones, and it seemed as if they would break if I pressed too hard. Her skin was smooth, almost slippery, as if the years had worn away all the roughness the way the wind wears away the surfaces of stones.

"Mike, Mike, I didn't think you'd come," she said, so happy, and she was still Ethel Barrymore, that voice like a caress. "I've been waiting all this time." Before I could reply, she looked away, out the window. "See the birds? I've been watching them at the feeder. I love to see them come. Even the blue jays. The blue jays are like hawks—they take the food that the small birds should have. But the small birds, the chickadees, watch the blue jays and at least learn where the feeder is."

She lapsed into silence, and I looked out the window. There was no feeder. No birds. There was only the parking lot and the sun glinting on car windshields.

She turned to me again, eyes bright. Radiant, really. Or was it a medicine brightness? "Ah, Mike. You look so grand, so grand. Is that a new coat?"

"Not really," I said. I'd been wearing my Uncle Jerry's old army-fatigue jacket for months, practically living in it, my mother said. But she insisted that I wear my raincoat for the visit. It was about a year old but looked new because I didn't wear it much. Nobody was wearing raincoats lately.

"You always loved clothes, didn't you, Mike?" she said.

I was beginning to feel uneasy because she regarded me with such intensity. Those bright eyes. I wondered—are old people in places like this so lonesome, so abandoned that they go wild when someone visits? Or was she so happy because she was suddenly lucid and everything was sharp and clear? My mother had described those moments when my grandmother suddenly emerged from the fog that so often obscured her mind. I didn't know the answers, but it felt kind of spooky, getting such an emotional welcome from her.

"I remember the time you bought the new coat—the Chesterfield," she said, looking away again, as if watching the birds that weren't there. "That lovely coat with the velvet collar. Black, it was. Stylish. Remember that, Mike? It was hard times, but you could never resist the glitter."

I was about to protest—I had never heard of a Chesterfield, for crying out loud. But I stopped. Be patient with her, my mother had said. Humor her. Be gentle.

We were interrupted by an attendant who pushed a wheeled cart into the room. "Time for juices, dear," the woman said. She was the standard forty- or fifty-year-old woman: glasses, nothing hair, plump cheeks. Her manner was cheerful but a businesslike kind of cheerfulness. I'd hate to be called "dear" by someone getting paid to do it. "Orange or grape or cranberry, dear? Cranberry is good for the bones, you know."

My grandmother ignored the interruption. She didn't even bother to answer, having turned away at the woman's arrival, as if angry about her appearance.

The woman looked at me and winked. A conspiratorial kind of wink. It was kind of horrible. I didn't think people winked like that anymore. In fact, I hadn't seen a wink in years.

"She doesn't care much for juices," the woman said, talking to me as if my grandmother weren't even there. "But she loves her coffee. With lots of cream and two lumps of sugar. But this is juice time, not coffee time." Addressing my grandmother again, she said, "Orange or grape or cranberry, dear?"

"Tell her I want no juices, Mike," my grandmother commanded regally, her eyes still watching invisible birds.

The woman smiled, patience like a label on her face. "That's all right, dear. I'll just leave some cranberry for you. Drink it at your leisure. It's good for the bones."

She wheeled herself out of the room. My grandmother was still absorbed in the view. Somewhere a toilet flushed. A wheelchair passed the doorway—probably that same old driver fleeing a hit-run accident. A television set exploded with sound somewhere, soap-opera voices filling the air. You can always tell soap-opera voices.

I turned back to find my grandmother staring at me. Her hands cupped her face, her index fingers curled around her cheeks like parenthesis marks.

"But you know, Mike, looking back, I think you were right," she said, continuing our conversation as if there had been no interruption. "You always said, 'It's the things of the spirit that count, Meg.' The spirit! And so you bought the baby-grand piano—a baby grand in the middle of the Depression. A knock came on the door and it was the deliveryman. It took five of them to get it into the house." She leaned back, closing her eyes. "How I loved that piano, Mike. I was never that fine a player, but you loved to sit there in the parlor, on Sunday evenings, Ellie on your lap, listening to me play and sing." She hummed a bit, a fragment of melody I didn't recognize. Then she drifted into silence. Maybe she'd fallen asleep. My mother's name is Ellen, but everyone always calls her Ellie. "Take my hand, Mike," my grandmother said suddenly. Then I remembered—my grandfather's name was Michael. I had been named for him.

"Ah, Mike," she said, pressing my hands with all her feeble strength. "I thought I'd lost you forever. And here you are, back with me again. . . ."

Her expression scared me. I don't mean scared as if I were in danger but scared because of what could happen to her when she realized the mistake she had made. My mother always said I favored her side of the family. Thinking back to the pictures in the old family albums, I recalled my grandfather as tall and thin. Like me. But the resemblance ended there. He was thirty-five when he died, almost forty years ago. And he wore a moustache. I brought my hand to my face. I also wore a moustache now, of course.

"I sit here these days, Mike," she said, her voice a lullaby, her hand still holding mine, "and I drift and dream. The days are fuzzy sometimes, merging together. Sometimes it's like I'm not here at all but somewhere else altogether. And I always think of you. Those years we had. Not enough years, Mike, not enough. . . ."

Her voice was so sad, so mournful that I made sounds of sympathy, not words exactly but the kind of soothings that mothers murmur to their children when they awaken from bad dreams.

"And I think of that terrible night, Mike, that terrible night. Have you ever really forgiven me for that night?"

"Listen . . ." I began. I wanted to say: "Nana, this is Mike your grandson, not Mike your husband."

"Sh . . . sh . . ." she whispered, placing a finger as long

and cold as a candle against my lips. "Don't say anything. I've waited so long for this moment. To be here. With you. I wondered what I would say if suddenly you walked in that door like other people have done. I've thought and thought about it. And I finally made up my mind—I'd ask you to forgive me. I was too proud to ask before." Her fingers tried to mask her face. "But I'm not proud anymore, Mike." That great voice quivered and then grew strong again. "I hate you to see me this way—you always said I was beautiful. I didn't believe it. The Charity Ball when we led the grand march and you said I was the most beautiful girl there . . ."

"Nana," I said. I couldn't keep up the pretense any longer, adding one more burden to my load of guilt, leading her on this way, playing a pathetic game of make-believe with an old woman clinging to memories. She didn't seem to hear me.

"But that other night, Mike. The terrible one. The terrible accusations I made. Even Ellie woke up and began to cry. I went to her and rocked her in my arms and you came into the room and said I was wrong. You were whispering, an awful whisper, not wanting to upset little Ellie but wanting to make me see the truth. And I didn't answer you, Mike. I was too proud. I've even forgotten the name of the girl. I sit here, wondering now—was it Laura or Evelyn? I can't remember. Later, I learned that you were telling the truth all the time, Mike. That I'd been wrong . . ." Her eyes were brighter than ever as she looked at me now, but tear-bright, the tears gathering. "It was never the same after that night, was it, Mike? The glitter was gone. From you. From us. And then the accident . . . and I never had the chance to ask you to forgive me . . ."

My grandmother. My poor, poor grandmother. Old

people aren't supposed to have those kinds of memories. You see their pictures in the family albums and that's what they are: pictures. They're not supposed to come to life. You drive out in your father's Le Mans doing seventy-five on the pike and all you're doing is visiting an old lady in a nursing home. A duty call. And then you find out that she's a person. She's *somebody*. She's my grandmother, all right, but she's also herself. Like my own mother and father. They exist outside of their relationship to me. I was scared again. I wanted to get out of there.

"Mike, Mike," my grandmother said. "Say it, Mike."

I felt as if my cheeks would crack if I uttered a word.

"Say you forgive me, Mike. I've waited all these years . . ."

I was surprised at how strong her fingers were.

"Say, '*I forgive you, Meg.*'"

I said it. My voice sounded funny, as if I were talking in a huge tunnel. "I forgive you, Meg."

Her eyes studied me. Her hands pressed mine. For the first time in my life, I saw love at work. Not movie love. Not Cindy's sparkling eyes when I tell her that we're going to the beach on a Sunday afternoon. But love like something alive and tender, asking nothing in return. She raised her face, and I knew what she wanted me to do. I bent and brushed my lips against her cheek. Her flesh was like a leaf in autumn, crisp and dry.

She closed her eyes and I stood up. The sun wasn't glinting on the cars any longer. Somebody had turned on another television set, and the voices were the show-off voices of the panel shows. At the same time you could still hear the soap-opera dialogue on the other television set.

I waited awhile. She seemed to be sleeping, her breathing serene and regular. I buttoned my raincoat. Suddenly she opened her eyes again and looked at me. Her eyes were still bright, but they merely stared at me. Without recognition or curiosity. Empty eyes. I smiled at her, but she didn't smile back. She made a kind of moaning sound and turned away on the bed, pulling the blankets around her.

I counted to twenty-five and then to fifty and did it all over again. I cleared my throat and coughed tentatively. She didn't move; she didn't respond. I wanted to say, "Nana, it's me." But I didn't. I thought of saying, "Meg, it's me." But I couldn't.

Finally I left. Just like that. I didn't say goodbye or anything. I stalked through the corridors, looking neither to the right nor the left, not caring whether that wild old man with the wheelchair ran me down or not.

On the Southwest Turnpike I did seventy-five—no, eighty—most of the way. I turned the radio up as loud as it could go. Rock music—anything to fill the air. When I got home, my mother was vacuuming the living-room rug. She shut off the cleaner, and the silence was deafening. "Well, how was your grandmother?" she asked.

I told her she was fine. I told her a lot of things. How great Nana looked and how she seemed happy and had called me Mike. I wanted to ask her—hey, Mom, you and Dad really love each other, don't you? I mean—there's nothing to forgive between you, is there? But I didn't.

Instead I went upstairs and took out the electric razor Annie had given me for Christmas and shaved off my moustache.

# Mine on
# Thursdays 🌿

# Introduction ✌

**M**ine on Thursdays" came into being on a Sunday afternoon in the fall of the year when I accompanied my daughter Chris, who was then about ten years old (she is at this writing twenty-two and a graduate student at American University in Washington, D.C.) to Whalom Park, an amusement park a short distance from our home.

On this particular Sunday, I was under assault by a migraine headache: a riveting pain in that vulnerable spot above my left eyebrow in partnership with nausea sweeping my stomach. But I'd promised to take her to the park and did so, pretending, to myself and to her, that I felt fine, just fine.

Our forays into the park were almost but not quite timid. She never showed any inclination to go on the more spectacular rides. For which I was grateful, having long ago lost any inclination toward those rides, if any inclination had ever existed.

That day, Chris was content to stroll the park, go on the merry-go-round and some of the other innocent rides while I watched as usual, delighting in her delight. We then wandered toward a new ride, something called the "Trabant," located near the Ferris wheel and midget motor cars. The Trabant was obviously a popular ride: the line was long. And Chris obviously wanted to try it. She said the kids at school thought it was "super." "But it's a little scary," she said. In repose, the Trabant looked docile enough, although

*she said the cars went "up, down and around." I remember
thinking that a ride that went up, down and around would
devastate me completely that day.*

*"Want to give it a whirl?" I asked, tentatively.*

*She looked brave in that heartbreaking way kids look
when they are attempting to be brave but aren't, really.*

*"Do you want me to go with you?" I asked, hoping she'd
say no.*

*She shook her head. Then, sighing deeply, she took the
plunge and we rushed for her ticket. The line had diminished, the attendant called "Hurry, hurry." We bought her
ticket; she took her seat and strapped herself in. I almost
joined her at the last minute. But didn't. Then the ride
started.*

*The next few minutes were excruciating. The ride was a
whirling, tilting nightmare. Dizzying, dazzling. And un-
ending. I caught occasional glimpses of Chris's face as her
car shot up and down and around. She held on for dear life.
Sometimes her eyes were tightly closed, other times they were
wide with horror. I stood helplessly by, trying to hurry time
along. Once, our gazes held for a split second, and it seemed
to me that I saw betrayal in her eyes. My betrayal of her. A
father wasn't supposed to abandon a child like that. Would
she ever forgive me?*

*The ride finally ended and she disembarked. She came
toward me on fragile legs, as if she were walking a tightrope.
Her hand trembled as I caught it. Was she avoiding my eyes?
I told her I was sorry, that I should have gone with her, that I
didn't think it would be so—so terrible. She assured me that
it wasn't that bad, that, sure, she'd been a little scared but it
was nothing, really, nothing. We both knew this was a
gentle lie. For my sake.*

*As we walked along hand in hand, the idea for the story*

*that eventually became "Mine on Thursdays" came forth. I had been thinking how lucky I was that our love for each other was so simple and secure that my betrayal—if that was the word—of her a few moments before did not threaten us. Yet, what if our love wasn't secure? What if that small betrayal in the park was only one more of many betrayals? What if it had been a final betrayal?*

*What if? What if? My mind raced, and my emotions kept pace at the sidelines, the way it always happens when a story idea arrives, like a small explosion of thought and feeling. What if? What if an incident like that in the park had been crucial to a relationship between father and daughter? What would make it crucial? Well, what if the father, say, was divorced from the child's mother and the incident happened during one of his visiting days? And what if . . .*

# Mine on Thursdays 🦋

To begin with, it took more than two hours to drive from Boston to Monument, twice the usual time, because of an accident near Concord that caused a traffic backup that turned a three-mile line of cars into a giant metal caterpillar, inching ponderously forward. Meanwhile, I had a splitting headache, my eyes were like raw onions and my stomach lurched on the edge of nausea, for which I fully accepted the blame. Ordinarily, the night before my Thursdays with Holly, I took it easy, avoided involvements and went to bed early. But yesterday afternoon, I'd had a futile clash with McClafflin—all arguments with employers are futile—and had threatened to quit, an empty gesture that caused him to smile because he knew about all my traps. This led to a few solitary and self-pitying drinks at the bar across the street, leaving me vulnerable to an invitation to a party in Cambridge, a party that turned out to be nothing more than pseudo-intellectual talk, plus liquor, the effect of which was pseudo: promising so much and delivering little except a clanging hangover and the familiar and desperate taste of old regrets. Somehow, I managed to survive the morning and left at my usual hour, aware that McClafflin was watching my painful progress through the office. And I thought: "The hell with you, Mac. You think I'm going to leave her waiting uselessly, while I take a cold shower and sleep it off. But Holly expects me and I'll be there."

I *was* there, late maybe but present and accounted for, and Holly leaped with delight when she saw me drive into her street. I made a reckless U-turn, knowing that Alison would be watching from the window, frowning her disapproval. The scarlet convertible in itself was sufficient to insult her cool gray New England eyes and my lateness was an affront to her penchant for punctuality (she'd been a teacher before our marriage and still loved schedules and timetables). Anyway, the brakes squealed as I pulled up in front of the house on the sedate street. On impulse, I blew the horn, long and loud. I always did things like that, to provoke her, killing myself with her, or killing whatever was left of what we'd had together, like a dying man hiding the medicine in the palm of his hand instead of swallowing the pill that might cure him.

Holly came streaking off the porch, dazzling in something pink and lacy and gay. Holly, my true love, the one person who could assuage my hangovers, comfort my aching limbs and give absolution to my sins.

"Oh, Daddy, I knew you'd come. I just knew it," she said, flinging herself at me.

I dug my face into her shampoo-scented hair and clutched the familiar geography of her bones and flesh. "Did I ever stand you up?" Then, laughing: "Don't answer that." Because there had been times, of course, when it had been impossible for me to come.

"Wonder World today, Dad?" she asked.

The sun hurled its rays against my eyeballs, penetrating the dark glasses, and the prospect of those whirling rides at the amusement park spread sickness through my veins. But aware that Alison was there behind the white curtains, I

assured Holly: "Whatever you say, baby, whatever you say."
Wanting Alison to know that somebody loved me. "The
sky's the limit."

Holly was mine on Thursdays, and during the two years
of our Thursdays together, we had made the circuit many
times—shopping trips to fancy stores, movie matinees,
picnics on Moosock Ridge, bowling, Wonder World in
season—all the things an adult can do with a child. I'd
always been careful to indulge her, basking in her delight.
We shared the unspoken knowledge that we were playing a
special kind of hooky, each of us a truant, she from that
well-regulated and orderly world of her mother's and I from
the world of too many martinis, too many girls, too many
long shots that had never come in.

For some reason, I thought of my father. Occasionally,
Holly and I journeyed out to the cemetery where I stood at
his grave and tried to recall him. I most often remembered
the time, a few weeks before he died, when we sat together
at the nursing home. After long minutes of silence, he'd
said: "The important thing, Howie, is to be a man."

He began to cry, tears overflowing his red-rimmed eyes,
and I pitied him, pitied all the old people who could only
look back, look back. After a while, I asked: "What's a man,
Dad?" Not really curious but wanting to say something.

My poor father. Who'd had too much booze and too
little love and no luck at all, at cards or dice or all those
jobs. And all the deals that had collapsed.

"To be a man," my father said, wiping his cheeks, "is to
look at the wreckage of your life and to confront it all
without pity for yourself. Without alibis. And to go on. To
endure—"

It had been a long day and I had been impatient to get
away from the ancient abandoned man who called himself

my father. I left shortly afterward, thinking: he'd always had a way with words, hadn't he? And what had it gotten him in the end? A wife whose early death had given him an excuse to drown himself in bottle after bottle, while his son, whose birth was the cause of that death, was shunted from uncle to aunt to cousin. Yet, he had tried hard to be a father, in his way, always showing up on holidays, bundled with gifts and stories of great adventures in the cities he visited on his sales routes.

Now, Holly and I drove along soft-shaded Spruce Street and I was relieved that a trip to the cemetery was not on the agenda that day. Holly chatted gaily. She told me about the neighborhood carnival she and her friends had staged and how their names had appeared in the newspaper because they'd donated the proceeds to charity. She described the shopping trips for school clothes, because September loomed ahead. She brought me up to date on all the things that make up the life and times of a ten-year-old girl, and I barely listened, taking pleasure in her presence alone. She wore pigtails, and she was dark, unlike Alison, who was blond, and this secretly delighted me. Holly prattled on: there was a fabulous new ride at Wonder World, "The Rocket Trip to the Moon," that all the kids were crazy about, and could we go on it, Dad, could we, huh, please?

"Why not?" I asked. All the "why nots" I had tossed her on Thursdays, like bouquets of love. I agreed so quickly because I knew she would change her mind at the last moment. Holly was shy, timid, and she usually avoided the more adventurous and perilous rides. Ordinarily, she was content to stroll through the park at my side while we made up stories about people passing by. She liked the merry-go-round and the distorted mirrors in the fun house and she was reluctant to attempt such daring exploits as the roller coaster or the loop-the-loop. For which I was grateful. Particularly on days such as this when my head pounded and my stomach revolted at the slightest movement.

"How's your mother?" I asked, the question ritual.

Usually, the answer was ritual, too. "Fine" or "swell." As if Holly'd received instructions. But today, she hesitated, sighed, and said: "Tired."

"Tired?" I was searching for a parking place in the busy Wonder World lot.

"Oh, she's been on a committee to get blood donors—"

That was Alison. Conscientious and community-minded and always willing to help. She had a desire for service to others and she dearly loved Monument and had no wish to venture to other places. Which was part of our trouble, or at least the beginning of it all. I had always regarded Monument as a starting point, not a destination. Alison and I had met the summer I'd been planning to leave, ready to knock on a thousand doors in New York City, seeking a job, something, anything—just to get away. But Alison had been so beautiful and I had loved her so incredibly that I'd remained in Monument, writing obituaries and other equally dismal stories for the town newspaper. However, I was always aware of the world outside of Monument and I had wanted to see it, to know a million people, visit a million places, all of which was ridiculous, of course, and eminently impractical. Sometimes, my frustration would burst out. "Alison," I'd plead, "let's try, let's pack up and take our chances. I don't mean go to the other side of the world. But somewhere. The world's so big and Monument's so small, our lives are so small—"

Alison had held up little Holly, who smiled at me in her infant innocence. "Is she so small, too, that you can't be a father to her?"

Defeated, I remained in Monument but spent more and more time away from that confining claustrophobic apartment. In a bar or cocktail lounge, there were kind shadows and when you'd consumed just the right amount of beer or rye or whatever, all the sharp edges blurred and Monument itself receded. Inevitably, if you go often enough to a bar, a girl walks in. And, finally, Sally arrived. She was a member of a television unit dispatched to Monument by a Boston station to capture, on tape, the one-hundred-fifth birthday of Harrison Shanks, the oldest man in the county. Sally and I had a drink or two; she confessed that she was only a secretary for the film crew, an errand girl, really. Laughing, she reversed the cliché and wondered what a fellow like me was doing in a place like that. Meaning Monument, of course. She leaned against me warmly, a frankness about her body. Alison hid herself in tailored suits or loose, comfortable sweaters while Sally wore clothes that made me constantly aware that she was a woman. Sitting beside her on that first night, before I had said two dozen words to her, I felt as though I had known her body before, probably in a thousand adolescent dreams.

The television people were in Monument only two days. I served as their unofficial guide, arranging the interview with Harrison Shanks, who sat bewildered in a wicker chair on the porch of his ancient house, croaking monosyllabic answers to the inane questions placed by the interviewer. "How does it feel to be one hundred five years old?" The old man, confused by time and place, kept muttering about the banks closing and Herbert Hoover, which caused a few laughs and quips off camera, and I felt myself tightening inside. Someone pressed my arm.

"You're a sensitive one, aren't you?" Sally asked.

"He's an old man. I've known him all my life."

"Poor boy," she said, touching the tip of my nose with a delicate finger. "You need a little tender loving care."

The interview with Harrison Shanks used up only ninety-three seconds of a special show dealing with the problems of the aged but my alliance with Sally lasted much longer than that. But not long enough. That was the terrible part: leaving Alison and Holly for Sally and all the bright promises of Boston, to dislocate our lives and make Holly that pitiable object—the child of a broken home—to do all that and then to end up alone, after all. Sally found other sensitive men upon whom to bestow her tender loving care. Her care wasn't really loving, I had learned, and I drifted from one job to another, sideways, not upward. To go upward demanded more than talent. It demanded ruthlessness and cunning, the necessity for sitting up nights plotting the next day's maneuver, the next day's presentation. But I found more allure in a drink or two, which became three or four, and then, what the hell, let's have a party, let's have some fun. And then it wasn't fun anymore.

"Daddy, you look kooky," Holly said now, giggling uncontrollably.

"You're not exactly Cinderella at the ball," I retorted.

We were regarding ourselves in the fun-house mirrors: Holly suddenly short and fat as if invisible hands had clapped her head down into her body, and I ludicrously tall and thin, pencil-like, my head a soiled eraser. Then we moved and exchanged grotesqueries, laughing some more at our reversed roles. At one point, I picked her up and whirled her around, basking in the gaiety of her laughter, despite the pain that stabbed my head. Dizziness overtook me and I set her down. "Let's rest awhile, baby." But she was carried on the momentum of her excitement and pulled me on. "The Rocket Ride, Dad, the Rocket Ride."

I let myself be led through the sun-dazzled park, telling myself to hold out for a little while. There was a small bar across the street and maybe I could duck in there for a cool one while Holly went on the rocket. On those Thursdays with Holly, I had seldom cheated that way, had devoted all my time to her, perhaps to show Alison that I wasn't completely without a conscience. When I had first called her after finding my loneliness intolerable, she'd been skeptical.

"We've been doing nicely, thanks," she said, cool and crisp. "Don't upset things, Howie. We haven't seen you for—how long? Three years?—and we've arranged our lives. It doesn't hurt anymore."

"You mean, you don't need me," I said.

When she didn't answer, I took the plunge. "But I need you."

Her laughter infuriated me. I wanted to hurt her. "All right, maybe not you. But Holly. I need her. She's mine, too. My blood runs—"

"I know. Your blood runs in her veins. But nothing else, I hope."

I was startled by her bitterness but, upon reflection, I saw that she was justified. When the divorce had become final, I hadn't made any particular demands about Holly. Alison had been generous enough to leave the terms open: I could see the child whenever and however I wished. Terms that I did not take her up on, because I was too intoxicated with my freedom and Sally and later the others. Until that day I called, alone and desperate in that hotel room, abandoned by everyone, needing somebody. And so we decided, over the telephone, that Holly would be mine on Thursdays. Thursday afternoon to be precise. Those first few weeks, I clutched at those hours with Holly as if they were gulps of oxygen in an airless world. We made the rounds, stiff and awkward at first, but finally Holly began to laugh at my jokes and eventually she accepted me. Alison remained distant, however, and never ventured out of the house. I was not invited inside, of course.

One day she addressed me through the screen door as I met Holly at the porch. She told Holly to go to the car.

"You know what you're doing?" she asked. But it wasn't a question: more an accusation.

"What?"

"Disrupting her life, her routine. Cruising in here every week like a year-round Santa Claus."

"Are you jealous? Or don't you think a kid needs a little fun now and then?"

She recoiled as if I'd slapped her or had stumbled upon the truth, and I felt a twist of triumph.

"Here we are, Dad," Holly said.

"My God," I cried, confronted by the huge and elaborate piece of machinery rising from the ground in front of us. Ordinarily, the rides in amusement parks all resemble one another, but the Rocket Ride seemed to be an exception, a roaring and revolving device that emitted billows of smoke and showers of sparks. Circular in design, the machinery contained small, simulated rockets with room for two or three people in each rocket. As the entire device moved in circular motion, the individual rockets swung up and down and occasionally poised daringly fifty feet above the ground before descending in a roar of smoke and flame. As we watched, the ride was apparently completing its circuit. I realized, finally, that the smoke was simulated and that the flames were actually paper streamers cunningly devised to resemble the real thing.

"Isn't it cool, Dad?" Holly asked.

I chuckled at my shy little girl, who had yet to find the courage for a trip on the roller coaster.

"You're not going on *this*, are you?" Although the ride was not as awesome as it had seemed at first glance, there was still that fifty-foot swoop.

"All the kids have," Holly said, eyes blazing with challenge. "If I don't, they'll think I'm—" she groped for the alien word—"chicken."

My poor sweet. So small and worried, risking an encounter with the monster to prove to her friends that she was not afraid. The ride came to a stop with screams and shouts and bellows and a muffled explosion. The pain between my eyes increased, my stomach rose.

"Please, Daddy?"

"Tickets," called the attendant.

"Boy, oh, boy," exulted a fellow coming off the ramp, his arm around a small blond girl who was flushed and excited, her body ripe and full. Somehow, our eyes met. She was young, but her eyes held the old message, the ancient code I had deciphered a thousand times.

"Can I, Daddy?" Holly's voice was poised on the edge of victory, interpreting my sudden preoccupation as acquiescence.

I watched the blond and her boyfriend as they made their way to a nearby refreshment stand. As a test. Sure enough, her eyes found their way to mine.

Holly had been leading me to the ticket booth, and I found myself with wallet in hand.

"You really want to go on this thing?" I asked, thinking that perhaps she had started to grow up, beginning to leave childhood behind. And yet I doubted her endurance. She was still only a baby.

"Oh, Daddy," she said impatiently, the woman emerging from the girl, a hint of the future.

I thought of a tall cool one in the bar across the street. Or maybe an approach to the blond. Handing a dollar to the cashier, I said: "One."

"Child or adult?"

"Child," I answered. Adult? What sane adult would risk a ride on that terrible parody of a rocket shot?

"Aren't you coming with me?" Holly asked.

"Look, Holly, your daddy's getting old for these kinds of capers. Rocket ships are for the young." Leading her toward the entrance, I urged: "Better hurry. You won't get a seat."

"Do you think I should go on the ride alone?" she asked, doubts gathering, almost visible in her eyes.

I squinted at the mechanism, conjuring up the vision of myself, complete with pounding head and queasy stomach, being tossed and turned and lifted and dashed down. Ridiculous. It was impossible for me to accompany her. I was not equipped for Rocket Rides, with or without a hangover. Blond or no blond.

The crowd jostled us, pushing forward, carrying us to the entrance. Placing the ticket in Holly's hand, I waved her on. She was swept along in the crowd and then emerged on the ramp leading to the platform where customers entered the individual capsules. The attendant on the platform took her ticket. I hoped he would realize how young she was and guide her to a rocket where other people would be near her. He led her to a small rocket, a capsule with enough room for only one person, installed no doubt for those who preferred to ride alone. She hesitated for a moment and then entered the compartment. She seemed small and wan and abandoned. She snapped a thin bar in place—her only protection from falling out. But, of course, nobody ever fell out of those things. Did they? I told myself to stop being melodramatic; it was only a lousy ride in an amusement park and she wasn't a child any longer.

Damn it. I walked over to the cashier's booth, drawing my wallet. But I was halted in my tracks by the attendant's cry: "All aboard. We're off to the moon."

"You can just make it, mister," the cashier offered.

But I'd look foolish scurrying up the ramp. And, besides, all the rockets were probably filled.

A belch of smoke escaped the rocket, the roar of an engine filled the air and the entire mechanism seemed to come alive. I ran back near the entrance, eager to see Holly before the ride began. She was sitting erect in her seat, as if she were a dutiful fifth-grader being obedient for her teacher. Her hands were folded in her lap. Our eyes met and I garlanded my face with a smile, assuring her that she was going to have fun. She nodded back, sighed a little, and with a roar and swish and boom, the trip started.

It all resembled a merry-go-round gone mad, the rockets whirling madly and individually, rising and falling and twisting, often at crazy impossible angles. I was grateful for my restraint, for having refused to go with Holly; I'd have been sick as a dog already. I glanced toward the refreshment stand; the blond was gone. Like so many others.

When I turned back to the ride again, it was in full swing. People screamed, those peculiar screams of terror and delight. The machinery *whooshed* and I sought Holly. At first, I couldn't find her in the nightmare of motion and color and sound. And then the small rocket swung into view and I spotted her. Her eyes were wide with surprise, her body tense, her hands clinging to the bar. Then she was gone, whisked away out of sight. The other people passed like blurs before my eyes. On the next turn, Holly's eyes were closed and her face resembled melted wax, as if a mad sculptor had molded her flesh into a mask of fright. As she began to rise, far up, I wondered whether there was an element of danger, after all. Suppose she lost her grip on the bar. I walked toward the attendant who stood at bored attention near the entrance, but I finally decided not to bother him. Stop dramatizing, I told myself. Then Holly swept by, her eyes wild with horror, terrible eyes, agonized. I hurried to the attendant and asked him how long the ride went on.

"What?" he shouted above the din.

"How long's the ride?"

"Five minutes. They get their money's worth," he yelled.

Stalking to my vantage point, I cursed myself. A moment later, she came into view, her eyes closed once more, her body crouched and tense, pitifully small and vulnerable. I remembered that as a child of three or so she'd been subject to nightmares. And she'd been afraid of thunder and lightning. I thought of all the thunderstorms she had endured and how I hadn't been there to comfort her.

Now, the rocket swept around again and began the long ascent. Her eyes were open, in a gaze of desperation. She looked downward and saw me. Her lips were pressed tight, her cheeks taut. In that precious moment, I tried to hold her in my view. I smiled, more than smiled: I attempted to inject courage and love and protection into my smile. And our eyes met for a long moment—and then she was gone. Up and away. Around and around. And I closed my own eyes.

The ride finally ended and I rushed to the exit to greet her, arms ready to welcome her, happy to have her safe at last. I watched as she carefully let herself out of the rocket. She walked, one foot after the other, across the ramp, a little unsteady, perhaps, but determined. I held out my arms as she approached.

"Holly!" I cried.

She looked up thoughtfully, startled, as if she were surprised to fine me there.

"Say, that was quite a trip, wasn't it?" I inquired. "Holy mackerel, I was ready to rip off my clothes, show my Superman outfit and leap to the rescue."

She smiled distantly. But not at my words. She was smiling at something else. It was a terrible smile. Private. The kind of smile that didn't belong on the face of a child.

"Are you all right?" I asked.

"I'm fine," she said.

"I'm sorry you were alone. Too bad you couldn't have gotten into a rocket with somebody else. I was afraid you might fall out."

"I'm safe and sound," she said.

But she wasn't looking at me.

"Well," I said, "what's next on the schedule?" Trying to induce enthusiasm into my voice.

"I think I'd like to go home, please," she replied, in her best polite-little-girl manner.

"It's early," I pointed out. "How about something to eat?" Ordinarily, she was ravenous for the things I bought her: popcorn and cotton candy and triple-header ice-cream cones.

"I'm not hungry," she said.

We were passing the fun house. I thought of those crazy mirrors inside and grimaced at the thought of myself bloated and distorted. With Holly walking beside me— beside me and yet getting farther and farther away with every step we took—I wondered if the mirrors weren't true reflections, after all. Forget it, I ridiculed myself, stop thinking of yourself as a poor man's Dorian Gray.

"Look, Holly, it's early. You said school's starting. How about a trip downtown? To Norton's? For some new clothes?" Everybody went to Norton's and I was sure that I would be able to charge purchases there without any fuss.

She blew air out of the side of her mouth. "I think I'd rather just go home," she said. "Besides, Mom isn't feeling too well. I might be able to help her."

"Your wish is my command," I said, keeping it light, keeping it gay.

And Alison. How tired did she get? And why wasn't she feeling well? Should I have inquired once in a while? But who inquired about me?

We made our way to the car under a sky suddenly subdued with clouds. The brilliance of the sun was muted, for which my eyes were thankful.

Once in the car, I asked: "Sure you want to go right home?" Clinging to her presence.

She looked straight ahead. I realized she hadn't looked at me directly since she'd emerged from the Rocket Ride.

"Oh, Daddy," she said.

*Oh, Daddy.* Without anguish, without any reprimand. *Oh, Daddy.* With a tired, weary acceptance that echoed a thousand other acceptances that had marked my life. A comment on all my defections.

"Next Thursday," I said, "we should do something different, something crazy." Thinking wildly. "Maybe your mother would let you come in to Boston. We could really do the town."

"I don't know," she said. "I think there's something

special going on next Thursday. At school. Orientation Day—getting ready for September."

"But—" I began. And then stopped. I'd been about to say: you are mine on Thursdays. But I saw, of course, that she was not actually mine, not on Thursdays or any other day of the week, or the year. We'd been playing truant, sure enough, but not as father and daughter, merely as adult and child. All those *why nots* I had tossed her—not bouquets of love, but bribes. I glanced at her as we drove along. She sat erect, composed, that elegance of Alison's so much in evidence, and I ached with love and longing and tenderness, knowing that she was more Alison than me, despite the dark hair. Where was I in her? Was I there at all?

I turned the car away from Spruce Street. "I'd like to drive by the cemetery," I told her.

"All right," she said, eyes still on the road ahead.

I stopped the car at the comfortless place of gray and green, slab and grass, and I thought of my father and what he had said that time about being a man and confronting the debris of your dreams. Without self-pity.

"Holly," I said.

Finally, she turned toward me—those lovely eyes, that curve of cheek. I had wondered before whether I was anywhere in her and now I hoped I wasn't.

"Yes?" she asked, mildly interested.

I wanted to say: "I'm sorry. I'm sorry for playing Santa Claus when I should have been a father. I'm sorry for wanting the whole world when I should have wanted only those who loved me. I'm sorry for the Rocket Ride—and all the Rocket Rides of your life that I didn't share."

Instead, I said: "I won't be coming to Monument for a while." I didn't allow her to answer but began to improvise quickly. "See, I've been thinking of leaving Boston, getting away from the rat race. I heard of a small-town newspaper up in Vermont—a weekly—that's looking for a man. Maybe I'll give it a whirl."

"That sounds interesting," she said, as if we were strangers on a plane.

"And if it works out, who knows? Maybe the Monument *Times* might have an opening someday."

*Don't you see, my darling, what I'm trying to say?*

"And I'll come home for good," I ventured.

She looked out over the cemetery, her face as bleak as any tombstone.

"Wouldn't you like that?" I asked.

At last, she looked at me again. "Yes," she said. For a moment, something raced across her face, something appeared in her eyes, perhaps an echo of the child I had known a long time ago. Then it faded. And the eyes were old. I knew I had done this to her. "Yes, that would be nice," she said, in that correct manner.

We drove away from the cemetery and to Spruce Street, and I parked in front of that house that once had been home. She kissed me dutifully on the cheek. I didn't blow the horn to provoke Alison or as a last attempt at amusing Holly. I drove away slowly, and I kept telling myself desperately that I wasn't saying goodbye.

# Another of
# Mike's Girls

# Introduction 🌿

*The* transient quality of adolescence and the emotional debris accumulated by adolescents along the way has always fascinated me. Not merely as an observer. I have carried my own emotional luggage from those adolescent years for a long long time. I still remember vividly the impact of a but—that monster of a word, as noted in "Another of Mike's Girls"—pronounced on the lips of a girl I was hopelessly in love with in the ninth grade: I think you're a swell guy, Bob, but . . .

I have always pondered a tragic law of adolescence. (On second thought, the law probably applies to all ages to some extent). That law: People fall in love at the same time— often at the same stunning moment—but they fall out of love at different times. One is left sadly juggling the pieces of a fractured heart while the other has danced away. We tell our sons and daughters: Don't worry, you'll get over it, nothing lasts forever, you won't even remember his (or her) name on your wedding day. But the anguish at the moment is devastating. The anguish finally leaves, but the echoes remain.

I never kept a scorecard of the emotional collisions of the teenagers in our family, but I was aware constantly of the various agonies and ecstasies taking place. I was also aware of my own part in these affairs. My position was on the sidelines. I was the audience. But it is possible for the audience to become emotionally tangled with the events taking place on stage.

All of this went into the writing of "Another of Mike's Girls." I knew all along I would write a story exploring the anguish that results when one person in a relationship cools toward the other. But I delayed writing the story because I was seeking another level. This other level requires further explanation.

Someone once said that poetry is saying one thing and meaning another. I have tried to apply that rule to my own writing, although I don't pretend to write poetry. But I'm interested in a second level in stories, a level that sometimes emerges vividly or, sometimes, subtly. I seldom begin a story until I see the possibility of this other level. There are times when I succeed in finding this other level; other times I fail.

In "Another of Mike's Girls," I am obviously writing about an adolescent love affair that ends when one of the pair falls out of love, as helpless to prevent it as he was helpless to prevent falling in love. This satisfied (for me) a situation I'd always wanted to explore. But the story held a deeper meaning for me, not only as the writer, but as a participant in the plot. Not really a participant because, most of the time, I, as the father of the adolescent, was invisible. Young lovers see only themselves, not the observer on the sidelines, a man trapped not only by his fixed place in the proceedings but by what placed him there and keeps him helpless: age.

This story, then, appears to be about another of Mike's girls and what happened to the girl and Mike. But I was really telling the story of Mike's father, and thus it becomes a story of a man reaching that moment when he realizes he is no longer young.

*The reader will eventually see why I titled the story
"Except When You're Shaving, Don't Look into Mirrors."
And the reader will probably also see why the editors retitled
it "Another of Mike's Girls."*

# Another of
# Mike's Girls 🥀

The trouble was that I saw her flaws before Mike did, and I was willing to accept them because she was, after all, a child really, a sophomore in high school, and I was not emotionally involved the way Mike was. At the end, I was invaded by pity, although I'm not sure for whom. However, at the beginning she was just another of his girls. Maybe I envied him, of course. I certainly envied his youth that late summer afternoon when he ran across the lawn as his friends called out raucous greetings from the car. The car was a scarlet MG, and it was unbelievable that it could hold that many people—it looked like some kind of monster with all those arms and legs sticking out. Mike's new girl was in the car. Ellie and I hadn't met her yet, she was too recent. Mike is always reluctant to introduce us to new girls because they come and go, and this week's movie date is often next week's memory. Then I caught a glimpse of her. She had extended her arms as if in supplication, and Mike disappeared into them and into the car. There was a flash of long dark hair and pretty face. Then the motor rocketed, drowning out the rock music issuing from the radio. They were off to the beach. Alex managed to squeal the tires as he backed out of the driveway—his dominant pleasure in life, apparently. At the last minute, Mike managed to wave goodbye.

"Lucky kids," Ellie said. Her voice surprised me; I thought she'd been in the kitchen doing dishes.

"If that madman Alex doesn't get them all killed."

"I wouldn't want to be eighteen again. Would you, Jerry?" she asked.

I thought of the car's swiftness and the shining beach and the splash of the waves and the inexhaustible energy and the girls in their bikinis. "I guess not," I said—without much conviction.

"Liar," she admonished, chuckling. "Don't tell me you've arrived at that dangerous age."

We have been married twenty-one years and she still has the ability to turn my knees liquid when she holds her head a certain way and looks at me.

"I've always been at a dangerous age," I said, giving her what passes for my Bogart grimace.

"I wonder what this one is like."

"Which one?" I asked.

"Mike's latest."

"Like all the others," I said.

All the girls Mike brought home looked alike. Long hair and short skirts. Or long hair and hip huggers. They were polite and pretty and had been pumped full of vitamins from the day of their birth and had started keeping dental appointments at the age of three or four. They were all entranced by the same songs on the Top 40, and they wore the same cologne. They had similar vocabularies—words like *gross* and *heavy*—and they prefixed almost every sentence with *like*. As a senior in high school, Mike majored in basketball, English and girls, not necessarily in that order, and I mention English because that's the only subject in which he receives an A on his report card. Although he's been on the varsity basketball squad since his sophomore year, the coach doesn't send him in too often—Mike's of average height, and he suffers in comparison with all those giants. But he's loyal and industrious and loves the game. One night last year he was sent in during the final moments, and he sank a beauty, the ball going through the hoop without touching the rim. He turned, searching the stands, and our eyes caught. He grinned, a grin that was a marvel of triumph and pride. For that quick moment, he was the boy I had taught to swim and fish, the boy with whom I took long walks on Saturday afternoons. The stands, with all the cheering fans, didn't exist for him. We were simply father and son, and the moment was all the more precious because I knew that this kind of sharing would become rarer and rarer. Why share moments like that with a father when the girls would be leaping and shouting?

As it turned out, the new girl was a basketball cheerleader. Her name was Jane, which was a change. I had been expecting something like Debbie or Donna or Cindy. Her hair streamed down to her shoulders; it was parted in the middle and stray strands kept falling across her eyes. She was sweet and well-mannered and her teeth were orthodontist-perfect and her favorite word was *wow*, which she pronounced with wonder and delight.

Mike was dazzled by her although, frankly, she was virtually a replica of the girl whose name I've forgotten that Mike had brought home a few weeks before. He couldn't keep his eyes off her, gulping her at every glance. He didn't mind the way she said *wow* about twice a minute. As in, "Wow, is that a heavy song." Or, "Wow, is that a neat sweater." She liked that word *neat* almost as much as *wow*. Embellish every sentence with the same recurring words, and the results can be nerve-racking, particularly if you hear it all from the next room where you're trying to concentrate on the new Maigret novel.

Actually, I was accustomed to the sounds of young people in the house. Annie brings her friends home from college for occasional weekends, and there's lots of singing and laughing. Julie is fourteen and brings home the younger set, and some of her girl friends merge into Mike's crowd. The telephone seems to ring all the time and the stereo plays frantically and the television is never mute. Ellie calls it "sweet racket," but it's only sweet to me when strained through a closed door.

Jane became part of the racket and the activity throughout the fall and on into the basketball season. Mike managed to play regularly—one of the Goliaths broke an ankle—and he scored his share of points. He'd drop his eyes modestly after making a basket, and Jane would leap in joyous triumph. There were five cheerleaders, and sometimes I couldn't tell her apart from the others.

Snow fell early, and they went off skating or skiing on weekend afternoons and evenings. "All that energy wasted on the young," I said to Ellie. Mike failed an important algebra test and received a warning card.

"Better talk to him," Ellie said.

And I did. He promised to do better, dismissing the subject quickly. "What do you think of Jane, Dad?" he asked. "Isn't she something?"

"Right now, I'd rather talk about algebra, Mike."

"I know, I know," he said, sighing. "And I know you're blaming my rotten marks on Jane and all the time I spend with her. Maybe I've been goofing off, but she's worth a warning card in algebra."

"Not to me, she isn't," I replied. "She's a sweet girl, Mike, but she's transient in your life. Here today, gone tomorrow. But your marks are important for the future—for college, scholarships. You can't afford to flunk subjects, Mike."

"She's not transient, Dad. I mean, she's here today, and she'll be here tomorrow."

"How long have you been going out with her?"

"Four months and three days," he said.

"That's some kind of record for you, isn't it?" I asked.

"She's keeping score," he said. "She reminds me every day." Although we were in touching distance, he was suddenly far away. "That Jane. She's really something . . ."

I had an opportunity to see her through Mike's eyes one Sunday afternoon when she poked her head into the den, blinked her eyes, smiled tentatively and said, "Hi, Mr. Croft."

I gave up my struggle with the newspaper and let the various sections fall like collapsed tents to the floor.

"May I come in?" she asked.

We had never exchanged more than pleasant greetings, and I studied her as she entered and then sat, Buddha-like, on the floor. Her long hair sparkled with cleanliness. As she pushed it back, I saw a constellation of acne on her forehead, but this only made her seem more human and less a model for shampoo on a television commercial. At Mike's age, I could have been dazzled by a girl like her.

"Well," I said, noticing finally that she carried a loose-leaf binder in her hands.

"Wow," she said, drawing out the word, like a sigh. "Mr. Croft, I know I shouldn't be bothering you, but . . ."

I tried to disguise my own sigh: I knew what she wanted. Although the company that employs me deals with art objects, and although I was an art major in college years ago, I am now involved in administrative affairs and have not touched brush or crayon for years.

She held out the binder. "I've got to show these to someone. Someone who *knows*, who's heavy in art. Like, my art teacher is a spaz."

"A spaz?"

"You know. Hopeless, a wipe-out."

And anyway, I thought, whether your teacher is a spaz or not, the way to a boy's heart is probably through the approbation of his father. I looked at her sketches. Landscapes. The same tree in every sketch. And everything perfect. But too perfect. The trees as alike as strings on a harp. Like painting by numbers. Yet she was obviously talented. Like thousands, millions of others. We talked awhile about her work, and I was encouraging, of course. It was a pleasant conversation. Her *wows* and *heavies* weren't as irritating when she flashed that smile at the same time.

"I really appreciate this, Mr. Croft," she said, getting up. "How can I thank you?"

By letting Mike get his mind back on algebra. But I said nothing, merely nodded at her appreciation.

Later, passing the kitchen doorway, I saw her with Ellie. They were discussing recipes. Jane was *wow*ing all over the place as Ellie described her special coffeecake recipe: The way to a boy's heart is also through his mother's kitchen.

But apparently Jane encountered a detour. At dinner a few nights later, Mike announced that he had volunteered to become photographer for the school yearbook.

"You actually volunteered for something that's got nothing to do with girls or basketball?" Julie asked.

Mike ignored her. "It's going to take up a lot of time, but my counselor at school thinks the extracurricular activity will help my scholarship chances."

"How about algebra?" I asked.

He had anticipated the question. "I got an A *minus* in this week's test and a B *plus* last week," he said.

"How about Jane?" Julie asked round-eyed. Nobody had yet asked her for a date, and she lived vicariously, following Mike's romances the way some housewives watch soap operas.

"What's Jane got to do with it?" Mike asked.

"Well, with basketball practice and this picture-taking stuff, when are you going to see her?" Julie asked, in a mild state of shock.

"Look, kid." He always called her kid when he was annoyed with her. "Jane's got her own life to lead. And anyway, I think a relationship needs room to breathe."

Julie had difficulty swallowing. "Boy, I never heard that one before."

Ellie came to the rescue: "Didn't Gibran say, 'Let there be spaces in your togetherness'?" With two teenage girls in the family, *The Prophet* is well-thumbed and much-quoted.

Ellie and I were familiar with Mike's pattern with girls, but in this case Julie had been the first to see it emerge. The process, however, is highly visible when his intentions become clear. Besides the new career in photography, Mike suddenly became very conscientious about homework. In addition, the basketball team became a possible entrant in the District Championship, which meant extra practice on weekends. "Can you imagine that, Jane? A chance to be the top team of all," I heard him telling Jane as I went by the telephone. There had been a time when all their phone conversations had been intimate, when he'd snake the cord into his room and close the door. Now he didn't mind standing in the front hallway in sight of anyone going by.

"How's Jane these days?" Julie asked, carefully casual at dinner that evening.

"Great," Mike answered. "Pass the potatoes, will you?"

"I haven't seen her around here lately," Julie persisted.

"We're going to the movies tonight," Mike said.

"Big deal," Julie snickered.

"What's that supposed to mean?" Mike asked.

But nobody answered. Everyone was busy eating, although I noticed that Mike didn't finish the steak that he usually devours, and he passed up dessert.

"What movie are you going to see?" Julie asked.

"I don't know," he said morosely, toying with his food. Ellie shot Julie a quick glance that said, Drop the subject.

Mike was still morose when he stalked into the house from the movie. He was early, which was unusual. Julie fluttered down the stairway, anticipating his return. "Mike . . ."

He held up his hand like a traffic cop, but she pressed on. "Did you and Jane have a good time?"

"I had a rotten time," he said.

"What happened?"

"Hey, Julie, lay off, will you?" he said.

Surprised at the anguish in his voice, I interrupted, reminding Julie that it was past her bedtime for a school night. She ascended the stairs with reluctant steps, muttering something about missing all the drama.

There was not much drama, really. Ellie had gone to bed early with a headache, and I had a data report to complete, and Mike banged around the kitchen, making the usual noise that accompanies his late-evening sandwich productions. After a while he emerged, carrying a sandwich in one hand and a quart of milk in the other. He sat down on the floor in the same Buddha-like pose Jane had assumed.

He took a bite of the sandwich and chewed without appetite: the condemned prisoner having his last meal.

"Know what's the matter with girls, Dad?"

"What?"

"They get on your nerves. Like Julie—poking her nose in everybody's business. And Jane. She's just great, but . . ."

"But what?" I asked, laying down the pencil.

"I don't know. Like, she combs her hair about a million times a day. Every time I turn around she's running a comb through her hair. And she's the kind of a girl that, if a song is playing on the radio, she sings along with it. And you can't really hear the song."

"She seems like a sweet girl," I offered.

"She is," Mike admitted. "She's just great, but . . ."

*But.* That monster of a word.

He pushed the sandwich aside; it was intact except for the half-moon that represented his only bite.

"It's all over between Jane and me," he said, finality in his voice like the slam of a door. "She wanted to know what had happened between us. And what could I say? I don't *know* what happened, Dad. I just . . ."

"You just don't feel the same way toward her," I said, trying to be helpful.

"Right," he said. "I feel like a rat . . ."

"You should feel like a rat," I said.

When he looked up in surprise, I said, "You can't help what happens to your emotions, Mike. Not at your age. Not at any age, I guess. It would be terrible to fake it with Jane or anybody else. If you didn't feel bad about it, you'd really be a rat."

He looked at me, and I felt again that fleeting moment of

sharing. It wasn't triumphant this time, like the basketball sinking through the hoop, but it was a sharing, anyway.

"Poor Jane," Ellie said later when I had brought her up to date.

"It was inevitable."

"I wonder what the next one will be like," she said.

"Like all the others," I said. "Except the next one will probably have another word instead of *wow.*"

I heard that *wow* again a week or so later when I stopped by a downtown drugstore for an evening newspaper.

"Hi, Mr. Croft. Wow! It's cold, isn't it?"

I didn't spot her at first. My glasses were fogged. And the stools at the soda fountain were occupied by teenagers wearing the same navy-blue jackets and faded jeans. But I'd have known that *wow* anywhere, and then I saw her waving.

Someone abandoned the stool next to her, and I sat down. "Hi," I said, groping for her name and then pinning it down: "Jane."

A sundae, strawberry apparently, stood before her; it looked regal and frigid and gaudy. I shivered from the cold that had followed me into the store, and she sat there, spooning ice cream into her mouth.

"How's your sketching going?" I asked, signaling the clerk for a cup of coffee.

"To tell you the truth, I haven't done much, Mr. Croft. Like, I'm not too ambitious. I guess I lack motivation." She sneezed and wiped her nose with a tissue.

"Well, you have plenty of time to develop ambition."

As usual, I burned my tongue on the coffee.

"How's Mike?" she asked.

"Fine."

"I hate myself," she announced, taking a huge bite of ice cream dripping with syrup. "I promised myself I wouldn't mention his name for at least six months, and here I am, wow, asking about him."

"Never hate yourself, Jane. You're too sweet a girl for that."

"Not many people think I'm sweet," she said, tossing her hair, revealing again the sprinkle of acne. She sniffed. "And I've got a cold on top of everything else."

I wondered: Where's the summer girl, the girl who went to the beach with Mike and splashed in the water, bikini clad and tanned and lovely?

"You're not a mess, Jane. You're pretty and talented. And someday you're going to knock some fellow off his feet."

She looked up, smiling wanly. "You're a nice guy, Mr. Croft."

Not really, I thought. I had been her enemy for a while because she had threatened Mike's scholarship. And I had gritted my teeth at all her *wows*. And I felt sad now about it all.

"I wish there were something I could do, Jane," I said, turning toward her. Despite the eyes that were bloodshot from the cold and the reddened nostrils, she was still lovely, those television commercial teeth and that shining hair. The sadness grew in me because I wished with all my heart that I could make her happy and knew there was no way for me to do so.

"There's nothing anybody can do, Mr. Croft," she said, "but thanks, anyway." She finished the sundae, licking the spoon, and then groped in her handbag for another tissue.

She got up from the stool and looked at me again, almost as an afterthought, as if she had forgotten my presence. And why not? I was Mike's father, not Mike. "Say hello to Mrs. Croft," she said, easing herself off the stool. "And to Julie."

I watched her walking toward the door: the faded jeans,

the long hair, the jacket emblazoned with a school name. You couldn't tell her from a million others. The sadness remained as I finished the coffee. I looked into the mirror and saw my reflection there: Mr. Croft, *you're a nice guy*, like a million others. I saw the lines like parenthesis marks enclosing the lips, the receding hairline, the small tugs of flesh beneath the eyes. And the wisps of gray in the hair. If all the young girls looked alike, then all the fathers looked alike too, didn't they?

I paid for the coffee, bought the evening newspaper on the way out and wondered whether I had been feeling sad all along for the wrong person. And I told myself: Except when you're shaving, don't look into mirrors any more.

# President Cleveland, Where Are You? 🌿

# Introduction 🌿

*T*here's a sentence in "President Cleveland, Where Are You?" which is probably the most significant I have written in terms of my development as a writer. The sentence echoes back to a lost and half-forgotten story I wrote in the days when I was scribbling stories in pencil at the kitchen table. The story was about a boy from the poorer section of a town who falls desperately in love with a girl from the other side of town where the people live, or so he thinks, grandly and affluently. The story was told in the first person, the narrator was a twelve-year-old boy.

The problem concerned description. The narrator (and I, the writer) faced the problem of describing the girl's house, a thing of grandeur and beauty, white and shining, alien to the three-story tenement building in which the boy lived. How to describe such a house? I knew little about architecture, next to nothing at all. The house had an aura of graceful antiquity—was it a relic of some earlier era? It seemed that I had seen such houses in books—but what books? I knew nothing about researching such a subject and, anyway, I didn't want to burden the narrative with a long description of the house. In fact, this would not only be fatal to the forward thrust of the story but would not be consistent with what a twelve-year-old boy would know about architecture. Yet, I wanted to describe it as more than just a big white house.

The problem brought the story to a complete halt. I walked

my hometown streets, desolated by the thought of all the things I did not know. How could someone so ignorant about so much ever become a writer? Back home, chewing at the pencil, I read and reread the words I had written. The lean clean prose of Ernest Hemingway and the simplicity of William Saroyan had affected me deeply, and I always told myself: Keep it simple, don't get too technical. So, let's apply those principles to the girl's house. Forget architecture— what did the house look like? Not what did it really look like, but what did it look like to this twelve-year-old boy?

Yes, that was the key—the viewpoint of the boy and not the writer. And from somewhere the description came. It looked like a big white birthday cake of a house! I knew this was exactly the kind of image I had sought. I felt the way Columbus must have felt when he sighted land.

In that moment, I had discovered simile and metaphor, had learned that words were truly tools, that figures of speech were not just something fancy to dress up a piece of prose but words that could evoke scene and event and emotion. Until that discovery at the kitchen table, I had been intimidated by much of what I encountered in books of grammar, including the definitions of similes and metaphors. Suddenly, the definitions didn't matter. What mattered was using them to enrich my stories—not in a "Look, Ma, how clever I am" way, but to sharpen images, pin down emotions, create shocks of recognition in the reader.

At any rate, the story of the boy and the birthday cake of a house has been lost through the years. I doubt if it was ever published. In "President Cleveland, Where Are You?" I resurrected the description. It occurs in the second sentence of the third paragraph, a tribute to a marvelous moment in my hesitant journey toward becoming a writer.

# President Cleveland,
# Where Are You? 🌀

That was the autumn of the cowboy cards—Buck Jones and Tom Tyler and Hoot Gibson and especially Ken Maynard. The cards were available in those five-cent packages of gum: pink sticks, three together, covered with a sweet white powder. You couldn't blow bubbles with that particular gum, but it couldn't have mattered less. The cowboy cards were important—the pictures of those rock-faced men with eyes of blue steel.

On those wind-swept, leaf-tumbling afternoons we gathered after school on the sidewalk in front of Lemire's Drugstore, across from St. Jude's Parochial School, and we swapped and bargained and matched for the cards. Because a Ken Maynard serial was playing at the Globe every Saturday afternoon, he was the most popular cowboy of all, and one of his cards was worth at least ten of any other kind. Rollie Tremaine had a treasure of thirty or so, and he guarded them jealously. He'd match you for the other cards, but he risked his Ken Maynards only when the other kids threatened to leave him out of the competition altogether.

You could almost hate Rollie Tremaine. In the first place, he was the only son of Auguste Tremaine, who operated the Uptown Dry Goods Store, and he did not live in a tenement but in a big white birthday cake of a house on Laurel Street. He was too fat to be effective in the football games between the Frenchtown Tigers and the North Side Knights, and he made us constantly aware of the jingle of coins in his pockets. He was able to stroll into Lemire's and casually select a quarter's worth of cowboy cards while the rest of us watched, aching with envy.

Once in a while I earned a nickel or dime by running errands or washing windows for blind old Mrs. Belander, or by finding pieces of copper, brass, and other valuable metals at the dump and selling them to the junkman. The coins clutched in my hand, I would race to Lemire's to buy a cowboy card or two, hoping that Ken Maynard would stare boldly out at me as I opened the pack. At one time, before a disastrous matching session with Roger Lussier (my best friend, except where the cards were involved), I owned five Ken Maynards and considered myself a millionare, of sorts.

One week I was particularly lucky; I had spent two afternoons washing floors for Mrs. Belander and received a quarter. Because my father had worked a full week at the shop, where a rush order for fancy combs had been received, he allotted my brothers and sisters and me an extra dime along with the usual ten cents for the Saturday-afternoon movie. Setting aside the movie fare, I found myself with a bonus of thirty-five cents, and I then planned to put Rollie Tremaine to shame the following Monday afternoon.

Monday was the best day to buy the cards because the candy man stopped at Lemire's every Monday morning to deliver the new assortments. There was nothing more exciting in the world than a fresh batch of card boxes. I rushed home from school that day and hurriedly changed my clothes, eager to set off for the store. As I burst through the doorway, letting the screen door slam behind me, my brother Armand blocked my way.

He was fourteen, three years older than I, and a freshman at Monument High School. He had recently become a stranger to me in many ways—indifferent to such matters as cowboy cards and the Frenchtown Tigers—and he carried himself with a mysterious dignity that was fractured now and then when his voice began shooting off in all directions like some kind of vocal fireworks.

"Wait a minute, Jerry," he said. "I want to talk to you." He motioned me out of earshot of my mother, who was busy supervising the usual after-school skirmish in the kitchen.

I sighed with impatience. In recent months Armand had become a figure of authority, siding with my father and mother occasionally. As the oldest son he sometimes took advantage of his age and experience to issue rules and regulations.

"How much money have you got?" he whispered.

"You in some kind of trouble?" I asked, excitement rising in me as I remembered the blackmail plot of a movie at the Globe a month before.

He shook his head in annoyance. "Look," he said, "it's Pa's birthday tomorrow. I think we ought to chip in and buy him something . . ."

I reached into my pocket and caressed the coins. "Here," I said carefully, pulling out a nickel. "If we all give a nickel we should have enough to buy him something pretty nice."

He regarded me with contempt. "Rita already gave me fifteen cents, and I'm throwing in a quarter. Albert handed over a dime—all that's left of his birthday money. Is that all you can do—a nickel?"

"Aw, come on," I protested. "I haven't got a single Ken Maynard left, and I was going to buy some cards this afternoon."

"Ken Maynard!" he snorted. "Who's more important—him or your father?"

His question was unfair because he knew that there was no possible choice—"my father" had to be the only answer. My father was a huge man who believed in the things of the spirit, although my mother often maintained that the spirits he believed in came in bottles. He had worked at the Monument Comb Shop since the age of fourteen; his booming laugh—or grumble—greeted us each night when he returned from the factory. A steady worker when the shop had enough work, he quickened with gaiety on Friday nights and weekends, a bottle of beer at his elbow, and he was fond of making long speeches about the good things in life. In the middle of the Depression, for instance, he paid cash for a piano, of all things, and insisted that my twin sisters, Yolande and Yvette, take lessons once a week.

I took a dime from my pocket and handed it to Armand.

"Thanks, Jerry," he said. "I hate to take your last cent."

"That's all right," I replied, turning away and consoling myself with the thought that twenty cents was better than nothing at all.

When I arrived at Lemire's I sensed disaster in the air. Roger Lussier was kicking disconsolately at a tin can in the gutter, and Rollie Tremaine sat sullenly on the steps in front of the store.

"Save your money," Roger said. He had known about my plans to splurge on the cards.

"What's the matter?" I asked.

"There's no more cowboy cards," Rollie Tremaine said. "The company's not making any more."

"They're going to have President cards," Roger said, his face twisting with disgust. He pointed to the store window. "Look!"

A placard in the window announced: "Attention, Boys. Watch for the New Series. Presidents of the United States. Free in Each 5-Cent Package of Caramel Chew."

"President cards?" I asked, dismayed.

I read on: "Collect a Complete Set and Receive an Official Imitation Major League Baseball Glove, Embossed with Lefty Grove's Autograph."

Glove or no glove, who could become excited about Presidents, of all things?

Rollie Tremaine stared at the sign. "Benjamin Harrison, for crying out loud," he said. "Why would I want Benjamin Harrison when I've got twenty-two Ken Maynards?"

I felt the warmth of guilt creep over me. I jingled the coins in my pocket, but the sound was hollow. No more Ken Maynards to buy.

"I'm going to buy a Mr. Goodbar," Rollie Tremaine decided.

I was without appetite, indifferent even to a Baby Ruth, which was my favorite. I thought of how I had betrayed Armand and, worst of all, my father.

"I'll see you after supper," I called over my shoulder to Roger as I hurried away toward home. I took the shortcut behind the church, although it involved leaping over a tall wooden fence, and I zigzagged recklessly through Mr. Thibodeau's garden, trying to outrace my guilt. I pounded up the steps and into the house, only to learn that Armand had already taken Yolande and Yvette uptown to shop for the birthday present.

I pedaled my bike furiously through the streets, ignoring the indignant horns of automobiles as I sliced through the traffic. Finally I saw Armand and my sisters emerge from the Monument Men's Shop. My heart sank when I spied the long, slim package that Armand was holding.

"Did you buy the present yet?" I asked, although I knew it was too late.

"Just now. A blue tie," Armand said. "What's the matter?"

"Nothing," I replied, my chest hurting.

He looked at me for a long moment. At first his eyes were hard, but then they softened. He smiled at me, almost sadly, and touched my arm. I turned away from him because I felt naked and exposed.

"It's all right," he said gently. "Maybe you've learned something." The words were gentle, but they held a curious dignity, the dignity remaining even when his voice suddenly cracked on the last syllable.

I wondered what was happening to me, because I did not know whether to laugh or cry.

Sister Angela was amazed when, a week before Christmas vacation, everybody in the class submitted a history essay worthy of a high mark—in some cases as high as A-minus. (Sister Angela did not believe that anyone in the world ever deserved an A.) She never learned—or at least she never let on that she knew—we all had become experts on the Presidents because of the cards we purchased at Lemire's. Each card contained a picture of a President, and on the reverse side, a summary of his career. We looked at those cards so often that the biographies imprinted themselves on our minds without effort. Even our street-corner conversations were filled with such information as the fact that James Madison was called "The Father of the Constitution," or that John Adams had intended to become a minister.

The President cards were a roaring success and the cowboy cards were quickly forgotten. In the first place we did not receive gum with the cards, but a kind of chewy caramel. The caramel could be tucked into a corner of your mouth, bulging your cheek in much the same manner as wads of tobacco bulged the mouths of baseball stars. In the second place the competition for collecting the cards was fierce and frustrating—fierce because everyone was intent on being the first to send away for a baseball glove and frustrating because although there were only thirty-two Presidents, including Franklin Delano Roosevelt, the variety at Lemire's was at a minimum. When the delivery-man left the boxes of cards at the store each Monday, we often discovered that one entire box was devoted to a single President—two weeks in a row the boxes contained nothing but Abraham Lincolns. One week Roger Lussier and I were the heroes of Frenchtown. We journeyed on our bicycles to the North Side, engaged three boys in a matching bout and returned with five new Presidents, including Chester Alan Arthur, who up to that time had been missing.

Perhaps to sharpen our desire, the card company sent a sample glove to Mr. Lemire, and it dangled, orange and sleek, in the window. I was half sick with longing, thinking of my old glove at home, which I had inherited from Armand. But Rollie Tremaine's desire for the glove outdis-̇tanced my own. He even got Mr. Lemire to agree to give the glove in the window to the first person to get a complete set of cards, so that precious time wouldn't be wasted waiting for the postman.

We were delighted at Rollie Tremaine's frustration, especially since he was only a substitute player for the Tigers. Once after spending fifty cents on cards—all of which turned out to be Calvin Coolidge—he threw them to the ground, pulled some dollar bills out of his pocket and said, "The heck with it. I'm going to buy a glove!"

"Not that glove," Roger Lussier said. "Not a glove with Lefty Grove's autograph. Look what it says at the bottom of the sign."

We all looked, although we knew the words by heart: "This Glove Is Not For Sale Anywhere."

Rollie Tremaine scrambled to pick up the cards from the sidewalk, pouting more than ever. After that he was quietly obsessed with the Presidents, hugging the cards close to his chest and refusing to tell us how many more he needed to complete his set.

I too was obsessed with the cards, because they had become things of comfort in a world that had suddenly grown dismal. After Christmas a layoff at the shop had thrown my father out of work. He received no paycheck for four weeks, and the only income we had was from Armand's after-school job at the Blue and White Grocery Store—a job he lost finally when business dwindled as the layoff continued.

Although we had enough food and clothing—my father's credit had always been good, a matter of pride with him—the inactivity made my father restless and irritable. He did not drink any beer at all, and laughed loudly, but not convincingly, after gulping down a glass of water and saying, "Lent came early this year." The twins fell sick and went to the hospital to have their tonsils removed. My father was confident that he would return to work eventually and pay off his debts, but he seemed to age before our eyes.

When orders again were received at the comb shop and he returned to work, another disaster occurred, although I was the only one aware of it. Armand fell in love.

I discovered his situation by accident, when I happened to pick up a piece of paper that had fallen to the floor in the bedroom he and I shared. I frowned at the paper, puzzled.

"Dear Sally, When I look into your eyes the world stands still . . ."

The letter was snatched from my hands before I finished reading it.

"What's the big idea, snooping around?" Armand asked, his face crimson. "Can't a guy have any privacy?"

He had never mentioned privacy before. "It was on the floor," I said. "I didn't know it was a letter. Who's Sally?"

He flung himself across the bed. "You tell anybody and I'll muckalize you," he threatened. "Sally Knowlton."

Nobody in Frenchtown had a name like Knowlton.

"A girl from the North Side?" I asked, incredulous.

He rolled over and faced me, anger in his eyes, and a kind of despair too.

"What's the matter with that? Think she's too good for me?" he asked. "I'm warning you, Jerry, if you tell anybody . . ."

"Don't worry," I said. Love had no particular place in my life; it seemed an unnecessary waste of time. And a girl from the North Side was so remote that for all practical purposes she did not exist. But I was curious. "What are you writing her a letter for? Did she leave town, or something?"

"She hasn't left town," he answered. "I wasn't going to send it. I just felt like writing to her."

I was glad that I had never become involved with love—love that brought desperation to your eyes, that caused you to write letters you did not plan to send. Shrugging with indifference, I began to search in the closet for the old baseball glove. I found it on the shelf, under some old sneakers. The webbing was torn and the padding gone. I thought of the sting I would feel when a sharp grounder slapped into the glove, and I winced.

"You tell anybody about me and Sally and I'll—"

"I know. You'll muckalize me."

I did not divulge his secret and often shared his agony, particularly when he sat at the supper table and left my mother's special butterscotch pie untouched. I had never realized before how terrible love could be. But my compassion was short-lived because I had other things to worry about: report cards due at Eastertime; the loss of income from old Mrs. Belander, who had gone to live with a daughter in Boston; and, of course, the Presidents.

Because a stalemate had been reached, the President cards were the dominant force in our lives—mine, Roger Lussier's and Rollie Tremaine's. For three weeks, as the baseball season approached, each of us had a complete set—complete except for one President, Grover Cleveland. Each time a box of cards arrived at the store we hurriedly bought them (as hurriedly as our funds allowed) and tore off the wrappers, only to be confronted by James Monroe or Martin Van Buren or someone else. But never Grover Cleveland, never the man who had been the twenty-second *and* the twenty-fourth President of the United States. We argued about Grover Cleveland. Should he be placed between Chester Alan Arthur and Benjamin Harrison as the twenty-second President or did he belong between Benjamin Harrison and William McKinley as the twenty-fourth President? Was the card company playing fair? Roger Lussier brought up a horrifying possibility—did we need *two* Grover Clevelands to complete the set?

Indignant, we stormed Lemire's and protested to the harassed storeowner, who had long since vowed never to stock a new series. Muttering angrily, he searched his bills and receipts for a list of rules.

"All right," he announced. "Says here you only need one

Grover Cleveland to finish the set. Now get out, all of you, unless you've got money to spend."

Outside the store, Rollie Tremaine picked up an empty tobacco tin and scaled it across the street. "Boy," he said. "I'd give five dollars for a Grover Cleveland."

When I returned home I found Armand sitting on the piazza steps, his chin in his hands. His mood of dejection mirrored my own, and I sat down beside him. We did not say anything for a while.

"Want to throw the ball around?" I asked.

He sighed, not bothering to answer.

"You sick?" I asked.

He stood up and hitched up his trousers, pulled at his ear and finally told me what the matter was—there was a big dance next week at the high school, the Spring Promenade, and Sally had asked him to be her escort.

I shook my head at the folly of love. "Well, what's so bad about that?"

"How can I take Sally to a fancy dance?" he asked desperately. "I'd have to buy her a corsage . . . And my shoes are practically falling apart. Pa's got too many worries now to buy me new shoes or give me money for flowers for a girl."

I nodded in sympathy. "Yeah," I said. "Look at me. Baseball time is almost here, and all I've got is that old glove. And no Grover Cleveland card yet . . ."

"Grover Cleveland?" he asked. "They've got some of those up on the North Side. Some kid was telling me there's a store that's got them. He says they're looking for Warren G. Harding."

"Holy Smoke!" I said. "I've got an extra Warren G. Harding!" Pure joy sang in my veins. I ran to my bicycle, swung into the seat—and found that the front tire was flat.

"I'll help you fix it," Armand said.

Within half an hour I was at the North Side Drugstore, where several boys were matching cards on the sidewalk. Silently but blissfully I shouted: President Grover Cleveland, here I come!

After Armand had left for the dance, all dressed up as if it were Sunday, the small green box containing the corsage under his arm, I sat on the railing of the piazza, letting my feet dangle. The neighborhood was quiet because the Frenchtown Tigers were at Daggett's Field, practicing for the first baseball game of the season.

I thought of Armand and the ridiculous expression on his face when he'd stood before the mirror in the bedroom. I'd avoided looking at his new black shoes. "Love," I muttered.

Spring had arrived in a sudden stampede of apple blossoms and fragrant breezes. Windows had been thrown open and dust mops had banged on the sills all day long as the women busied themselves with housecleaning. I was puzzled by my lethargy. Wasn't spring supposed to make everything bright and gay?

I turned at the sound of footsteps on the stairs. Roger Lussier greeted me with a sour face.

"I thought you were practicing with the Tigers," I said.

"Rollie Tremaine," he said. "I just couldn't stand him." He slammed his fist against the railing. "Jeez, why did *he* have to be the one to get a Grover Cleveland? You should see him showing off. He won't let anybody even touch that glove . . ."

I felt like Benedict Arnold and knew that I had to confess what I had done.

"Roger," I said, "I got a Grover Cleveland card up on the North Side. I sold it to Rollie Tremaine for five dollars."

"Are you crazy?" he asked.

"I needed that five dollars. It was an—an emergency."

"Boy!" he said, looking down at the ground and shaking his head. "What did you have to do a thing like that for?"

I watched him as he turned away and began walking down the stairs.

"Hey, Roger!" I called.

He squinted up at me as if I were a stranger, someone he'd never seen before.

"What?" he asked, his voice flat.

"I had to do it," I said. "Honest."

He didn't answer. He headed toward the fence, searching for the board we had loosened to give us a secret passage.

I thought of my father and Armand and Rollie Tremaine and Grover Cleveland and wished that I could go away someplace far away. But there was no place to go.

Roger found the loose slat in the fence and slipped through. I felt betrayed: weren't you supposed to feel good when you did something fine and noble?

A moment later two hands gripped the top of the fence and Roger's face appeared. "Was it a real emergency?" he yelled.

"A real one!" I called. "Something important!"

His face dropped from sight and his voice reached me across the yard: "All right."

"See you tomorrow!" I yelled.

I swung my legs over the railing again. The gathering dusk began to soften the sharp edges of the fence, the rooftops, the distant church steeple. I sat there a long time, waiting for the good feeling to come.

# A Bad Time for Fathers 🌱

# Introduction 🌿

**W**hen the story that follows *appeared in* Woman's Day, *it carried the title "A Bad Time for Fathers," a drastic departure from its original title, "The Indians Don't Attack at Dawn Anymore." I accepted the change philosophically, thinking that an apt title for a certain aspect of my writing career could be called "A Bad Time for Titles."*

*Most of my titles arrive in a flash, usually about the time the idea of the story comes to life. Because the titles are with me during the entire experience of writing, any change is unsettling. It's as if you called your child John while he was growing up and, suddenly, when he begins school, the teacher calls him George. George may be fine—but you named him John.*

*I don't try to be perversely flamboyant with titles, although I must confess a weakness for long ones. Yet, could any title be shorter than "The Moustache?" Why should a title always be brief and obvious? Why not a title that seems obscure, although it evokes the mood of the story? A story I once wrote has a title that sets the tone of the story— "Charlie Mitchell, You Rat, Be Kind to My Little Girl"— light, direct, but with a hint of poignance in those last three words,* my little girl. *Or so it seems to me.*

*The question arises: What's a good title, anyway? What's it supposed to do? Arouse curiosity, compel the reader to begin reading at once, hint gently at what is to come, or spell* out to the reader exactly what awaits? I'm not sure. In fact, I even contradict myself on occasion. "The Indians Don't Attack at Dawn Anymore" certainly doesn't convey the plot or the theme of the story. It's not about the end of the Indian wars. Yet, it's about the end of something only gently indicated, and the reader will learn what that something is eventually. I think the reader receives a pleasant shock of recognition when, suddenly, the meaning of the title becomes clear as the story is being read. I love that kind of surprise in stories and, frankly, I try to write the kind of stories I would enjoy reading.

There's a big difference between titling a book and titling a story. For one thing, magazine editors don't advise me when a title change has been made. I learned about "A Bad Time for Fathers" when I opened the magazine. Book titles are discussed at length, are even researched to see if other authors have used them. The title is usually decided upon long before the manuscript goes to the printers.

Perhaps I'm sensitive about the subject because my first published novel—few events can compare with the publication of that first novel—was retitled by the publisher. The novel was about a man dying of cancer, and my title had been Every Day They Die Among Us from a W. H. Auden poem which contained the following:

> Of whom shall we speak? For every day they die
> Among us, those who were doing us some good,
> And knew it was never enough but
> Hoped to improve a little by living.

This was such a perfect reflection of the story that I was dismayed when the publisher said my title couldn't be used. Why? Because it contained the word die. Die is a downer. But the novel was about dying. Yes, the publisher said, but we must avoid the word because it would discourage people from reaching for the book. Eventually, the publisher settled on Now and at the Hour which was a reasonable choice, I suppose, because it has a certain ominous ring and it also derives from a Catholic prayer: "Pray for us now and at the hour of our death." Thus, it evokes the aura of death without using the word. Clever. But someone else had baptized my child. I vowed to fight for my titles in the future. Which I have done, when given the chance.

The only other title change in this collection concerns the story that appeared in McCall's as "Another of Mike's Girls." Here again, I learned about the change when I turned to the index on the day the magazine arrived. The original title was "Except When You're Shaving, Don't Look into Mirrors." Frankly, I didn't expect McCall's to keep the original, but how I loved it—and still do.

"A Bad Time for Fathers" was written when I was feeling sentimental about the imminent departure of our oldest daughter, Bobbie, to college. The trick was to write the story with feeling but without sentimentality. The party in the story never occurred, and the character of the boy friend, Sam, is a complete fabrication, although I myself have been Sam in a thousand manifestations.

# A Bad Time for Fathers 🌿

Probably the party had been a mistake, after all, because it provided a focus for the farewells, a time and place to say goodbye, the kind of thing "The Imp" disliked intensely. (She wasn't "The Imp" anymore, either, but simply *Jane*, startlingly formal, almost regal at unexpected moments.) Anyway, it had started out as a small gathering of girls, all of them leaving for college or jobs out of town, an informal get-together at summer's end, with hamburgers and hot dogs, and probably some activity in the backyard—horseshoes ("So square, Dad"), or croquet, which she didn't consider square at all because she was expert at the game. But it turned into a party simply because Ellen loves to get her hands on a menu and an invitation list and all the rest of it. What we didn't realize, Ellen and I, was that the party emphasized Jane's departure. If we had avoided an official event and merely driven her to college on Sunday, then her entrance into another way of life wouldn't have been so marked, so jagged in our hearts.

All of which, of course, was much too dramatic for her. And corny.

"Look guys," she said, "I'm only going to college. In Boston. I'll only be a hundred miles away, for crying out loud." She called everybody guys. Even girls.

"A hundred twelve," I said.

But she finally relented and allowed Ellen to proceed

with plans for a big affair with all the trimmings. And that brought up a sudden problem.

"That means Sam," she said.

"Why not Sam?" I asked, surprised.

She paused. She'd started pausing dramatically, lately. "He's an epilogue, Dad."

"Epilogue? The only epilogues I know about are in books."

She blew air out of the corner of her mouth, which meant that she was being very patient with me.

"I mean," she said, "an epilogue is something that happens *after* the end of the story."

I should have sighed with relief, I suppose. After she'd met Sam at the Senior Class Christmas Dance and began to spend most of her time with him—her homework suffering dangerously for a while—Ellen and I had been concerned. Jane seemed so young and vulnerable; Sam was tall and energetic and, although he was polite, he seemed aloof and remote, removed from our world. He was only a teenage boy, I reassured Ellen. They're all remote. He also was accident-prone, a potential demolisher of houses. Probably cities. During his first visit, he politely admired one of Ellen's bone-china cups and saucers and somehow dropped the cup, which shattered, of course, beyond repair. "Oh, that's nothing," Jane had said, blithely dismissing the incident as Ellen turned away, stricken. Jane had also worn a crazy ring Sam had won at a carnival. It turned her finger green at first, then purple. But she continued to wear it long after I had envisioned an amputation to save her life.

Now, suddenly, Sam was an epilogue. But she invited him anyway, and he arrived late, as usual.

The party coincided with one of those leaf-toasted afternoons when late summer conspires with early autumn to produce an in-between period of grace and loveliness. The fellows and girls spread themselves around the house and across the lawn. Ellen had arranged a buffet, setting out tables beneath the old maple in the backyard. In the days when Jane was still "The Imp," one branch of that tree had held her first rope swing. She had planted her first radishes in a patch of land near her Tom Sawyer fence. It turned out later that she couldn't stand the taste of radishes. Her Tom Sawyer fence had been a disaster, too. She'd offered to paint the fence for me for five dollars, figuring she would inveigle her friends into doing the work. But the plan had backfired. I had watched her painting for a while; she always curled her tongue around the corner of her lips when she concentrated fiercely. The fence seemed suddenly endless in its length and I went out to help her. "No," she said with ten-year-old determination, "a bargain's a bargain, Dad." Abandoned by her friends (who, as it turned out, had naturally read *Tom Sawyer*, too), she completed the job alone. And I had felt sad watching her, not knowing exactly why.

Now she leaned against that fence, serene and secure among her friends, laughing and smiling and tossing her head. Croquet balls clicked against each other, sounding like giant dice, and badminton corks sailed like captive birds across the net. Ellen was busy dispensing food and drink with the aid of some neighborhood mothers. People nodded absently at me, as if they weren't sure whether I'd wandered into the party by mistake. I went into the house, finding my way through the clusters of fellows and girls and mixed my own drink, definitely not for teenagers, inviting its chilling dryness to mellow my mood.

Somehow I heard the doorbell above the buzz and chatter. It was Sam. He was perspiring. I had noticed from the beginning that he had a tendency to sweat in the mildest of weather or even while playing croquet, and that he always reeked of some sharply spiced and terrible deodorant or after-shave lotion. Jane hadn't noticed things like that. She kept talking about his eyes, how soft and kind they were, how they sometimes crackled with excitement. *Eyes crackling?* Which sent her off to her room in a huff: "Oh, Dad, you're making fun." Now Sam arrived, late, a bit out of breath, still tall but somehow awkward now in his tallness. He stood tentatively at the door. I approached him warily, bracing myself for the assault of his aroma.

"Hi, Mr. Croft," he said, his eyes searching elsewhere. "Cripes, I know I'm late. I had trouble with the carburetor. And I had to work an hour overtime at the store." Suddenly, he was heavy with woe. In other times, he could do no wrong, had been a glamorous figure, even though he hadn't made the basketball team. Something about weak ankles that buckled at odd, unexpected moments.

"But basketball is superfluous anyway," Jane had said, "superfluous" having been her favorite word at the time. Now, he had bad luck with the car and Jane had other favorite words, "epilogue" among them.

"You haven't missed a thing, Sam," I said. "She's out back somewhere." He smelled of lemon, which was an improvement over the banana aura that had surrounded him the last time he dropped around.

Waving him off, I made my way to the stairs, carrying my glass, tired suddenly of the noise, and in particular the raucous record that was beginning its ten-thousandth orbit on the stereo. Jane's room looked down on the backyard. Ordinarily I stayed out of the place because it presented a formidable landscape: a mess. Posters taped to the wall, everything helter-skelter, strewn shoes and books and other stuff that turned the floor into a relief map you had to step cautiously across. "Would you please, repeat, please clean up that room," had been her mother's cry through the years.

"Right, Mom," Jane would answer. But she never did.

The view from the window was magnificent. The backyard trailed off into a long field that disappeared into Moosock Brook somewhere. In the distance, autumn hills looked like collapsed wigwams. When Jane was a child, we sat at this window and I'd tell her about the tribes who'd held their powwows on Mount Wachusum and then galloped their horses across the plains to attack the cabins of the early settlers. Late on a smoky afternoon you could almost see the dust of horse hooves rising in the distance.

"Hey," she said, "why not join the party?"

Without waiting for my reply, she swept into the room, miraculously managing to avoid tripping on the floor's accumulation. "They want more records," she said, bypassing the empty record rack and rummaging under the bed.

Arms embracing records, she halted in her departure. "What are you doing, Dad?"

Indicating the horizon, I said: "Looking for some Indians." The martini had something to do with the answer.

"At this hour of the day?" Amused, indulgent, she said, "They attack at sunrise."

But she wasn't playing the game, really. Her cheeks were flushed and her eyes party-bright. I wanted to detain her anyway.

"A few days from now, Jane, you'll be on your own. Living in a dorm. Know how you like privacy? Well, you'll be stuck in a dorm with—what?—three hundred other freshmen under one roof." I glanced around the room, shuddering with simulated horror. "All those teenage girls living together. It's like this place multiplied three hundred times."

"But you miss the point, Dad. The point is, this room isn't really a mess. It's comfortable. *Parents* think rooms are messes. So, at school, with no parents around—no messes." She juggled the records in her arms.

"No parents," I mused. "That sounds chilling."

"Dad, Dad, know what you are? A character. I'm not going to Mars."

"Distance is a funny thing," I said. "When you went to Girl Scout camp, you were only thirty miles away, but homesick. You sneaked out of the place and called us—collect, incidentally—pleading for rescue."

"I was twelve years old, for crying out loud."

"But that was only five or six years ago."

"Hey, Dad. Have you looked at me lately?"

"That's what hurts, baby," I thought. "I've looked at you too much lately and can't find the homesick Girl Scout whose uniform never seemed to fit right."

Turning to the window, I saw a wandering figure below. "There's Sam."

She made an effort to peer into the backyard. "I know," she sighed.

We watched Sam trying to negotiate his way under a badminton net while balancing a paper plate that contained two hamburgers, a hot dog, a bottle of soda pop and a pile of potato chips.

"The thing is," she said, frowning as if puzzled about something, "that he's such a good guy. Really great. He's got this way about him that knocks me out: he always acts as if he's protecting me. Like, he always holds my elbow when we cross the street." She continued to look down at him, pensive, almost sad. Then, brightly: "We learned in school that man is the most adaptable of all species."

"What has that got to do with Sam?"

That patient whistle of air again. "I mean, Sam will get used to it."

"Does he know that?"

"Of course. We talked. Do you think I'm such a rat? He's going away, too, Dad. We've both got everything ahead of us. A new life, new people. We've both got to be free."

Smoke rose from a distant hill. Harry Arnold burning his leaves. "Look," I said, touching her shoulder. "Indians. On the warpath."

"That's Mr. Arnold burning his leaves," she said. And, turning away, "I've got to go, Dad. They're waiting."

After her departure, my eyes sought Sam across the lawn. He had found a quiet spot, and was preparing to sit on one of those wrought-iron garden chairs, white and decorative and stylish, but definitely fragile, definitely not for sitting. Not the way his luck had been running recently. I had assembled the chair myself in the spring, and I have always been lousy at tightening nuts and bolts. But he sat down, and nothing happened. One for Sam's side.

Seeking a refill for my glass, I encountered Ellen in the kitchen. She was doing something or other with a wild assortment of food.

"Thank goodness I ordered this extra stuff," she said. "Did you ever see anybody eat like this? But everything seems to be going fine, doesn't it?"

"Yes," I said.

She paused. "What's the matter?"

"Nothing."

"Kids getting on your nerves? All the racket? How can they stand that music—two stereos going at once! Are you feeling all right?" She could always keep several topics going in one conversation, like a verbal juggler.

"Ellen," I said, as we were jostled by an invasion of fellows and girls sweeping through the kitchen to the living room.

"What?" she asked, preoccupied as she tested the dip she had just concocted.

"Why should I be feeling sorry for Sam? Sam, of all people."

"Is that what's the matter?" she asked, evidently satisfied with the taste of the dip.

"Not too long ago I couldn't stand the sight of him."

"You're a compassionate man," she said.

"Not that compassionate. You ought to get a whiff of that after-shave he's wearing today."

But she was carried away in a tide of guests. Holding the tray aloft, she cried: "Careful, it'll spill."

I almost tripped over a croquet wicket as I crossed the backyard, heading for no place in particular. Eventually, I found my way to Sam.

He leaped up with alacrity. Once he had walked across my living room as if he were making the mortgage payments. Now, he attempted a pathetic smile, his cheeks bulging with whatever terrible mixture he had crammed into his mouth. My nostrils made tentative inquiries: at least he had bypassed the onion.

"Food good?" I asked.

His throat rippled as he swallowed the gigantic mass. "Beautiful," he said. "Actually, I haven't been too hungry lately. But I rushed here straight from work and didn't get a chance to eat. I mean, I actually haven't eaten since seven o'clock this morning."

I wasn't too interested in his eating habits and so the

conversation languished. We watched them playing croquet. A few couples were dancing on the patio. I realized a silence had deepened between us despite all the racket that filled the air.

"How do you feel about college?" I asked.

He mumbled something that sounded like "swell."

"Let's see. You'll be up in New Hampshire, right?"

"Right," he said, exhaling.

Maybe he'd had onions after all.

I spotted Jane strolling along the side of the house, chatting and laughing with somebody or other. I had long since stopped trying to sort out the guests.

Turning at a horseshoe's clamor and the shout of "ringer," I caught sight of Sam looking at her. There was such anguish, such longing in that face. We both watched her progress through the yard, sprightly in her loveliness, animated, filled with grace and good humor, at ease with the world. You bring up your children to be self-reliant and independent and they double-cross you and become self-reliant and independent.

"Sam," I said, turning back to him.

"Yes, Mr. Croft?" The words came out as if they'd been printed on a slip of paper and memorized.

"New Hampshire isn't that far from Boston."

His reply was lost in a cry from the other side of the patio: "Let's choose up sides." We moved into the area of activity where a game was being organized, something that consisted mostly of wild giggles and laughter. I made my way toward the back door, slowly. The day suddenly looked tired. The leaves of the maple seemed limp, the colors subdued. I could imagine grass blades folding into each other. Ridiculous: I seemed to be the only one who was tired.

In the kitchen, Ellen was attacking the dishes, helped by the neighborhood friends. Their talk was animated and meaningless. I found a quiet spot in the den and closed my eyes, allowing myself to float away.

"Mr. Croft?"

The voice came from a far distance. Pulling myself from sleep, I looked up at Sam.

"I'm going," he said. "I figured I'd say goodbye. I mean, I'll be leaving for college myself on Monday so probably I won't be around for a while."

Rising to my feet, I realized that evening had become night while I slept. The chemistry of the party had changed. Departures echoed in the air. Subdued talk filtered in from outside.

"Well, Sam, it's been fine having you here," I said, groping for words. I had not envisioned a farewell scene.

"Thanks for everything," he said, as I accompanied him through the dining room and the living room to the front door. Sprinkles of laughter reached us from outside, with quiet pauses now and then. I reached for a light switch but wasn't quick enough. Sam had already tripped and as he pitched forward his hand lashed out and brought down a lamp base: base, shade and all crashing to the floor. The bulb burst as if an invisible photographer were taking our picture.

Sam was profuse with apologies as we groped around on our knees in the dark. "Forget it, Sam," I said, "it was an accident."

The overhead light went on, snapped into brilliance by Jane. I looked up at her, feeling silly.

"You two," she said, hands on hips, shaking her head, vastly amused by it all.

"Look," I began, rising to one knee. I was about to say:

"Look, my dear, I am your father. I changed your diapers and signed your report cards. Don't link me with this stumbling bumbling schoolboy." *You two.* But I realized that Sam and I were more than conspirators over a broken lamp. I had been using him for camouflage.

A horn blared outside.

"Somebody's leaving. I've got to say goodbye to them," Jane said. And she was out the door.

"Jeez, Mr. Croft," Sam said, "how much did the lamp cost?"

"Only money," I answered, with the famous nonchalance no one knew I was famous for.

After picking up the pieces and restoring order, I finally got him to the door.

"Sam," I said.

He regarded me wearily, as if I were about to hand him a bill.

"Sam, before a girl can come back, she has to go away first. Know what I mean?"

He looked at me for a long time and then lifted his shoulders and did something with his elbows and smiled and frowned and coughed, all at the same time. I vowed to avoid future encounters with adolescents. The final wave of departing guests engulfed us in the hall and Sam was carried along with them. I had been unable to say what I'd needed to say: "This is a bad time in her life for either one of us—lover or father." But he might have flung his arms out and broken another lamp, anyway.

I could hear Jane outside, shouting goodbye to people, distributing her farewells. "Goodbye, Sam," she called.

Silently, I amended that statement to Sam: "A daughter has to go away for a while before she can come back." I wished I could have said it aloud to make it sound more convincing.

In the kitchen, Ellen started the garbage disposal and, as usual, every pipe in the house began to rattle. I stood for a moment looking at the broken lamp and the other remnants of the party. After mixing myself another drink, I went upstairs to see if there were any Indians riding to attack, although I knew that they were gone forever.

# Protestants Cry, Too

# Introduction 🌿

*I* *am assuming that the reader has read "President
Cleveland, Where Are You?" before embarking on these
remarks because there is such a distinct relationship between
that story and "Protestants Cry, Too." The stories are very
much alike and yet distinctly different. Let me explain.*

*The setting of both stories is Frenchtown, the French
Canadian section of a small New England city, the time is
the 1930s Depression, and the cast of characters is almost
identical. The narrator of both stories is a boy named Jerry;
Armand, a high school student, is his older brother; Roger
Lussier is Jerry's best friend; Sister Angela presides in the
classroom; the Globe Theater is their palace of celluloid
dreams; Jerry's father works in the comb shop. An important
part of both stories is the fact that Armand is in love with a
girl from the other, more affluent, side of town.*

*Thus, the similarities. The differences? Subtle, perhaps,
but so unmistakable that it seems to me that "Protestants
Cry, Too" hardly fits into the Depression era stories in this
collection. It has a certain aura, a sense that it belongs to a
time far removed from the Depression. The family, although
American (the father is proud of his citizenship and is a
partisan of Franklin Roosevelt), is more Canadian in spirit,
more recently arrived from Canada, more alien to the
American way of life. Would the father in "President
Cleveland, Where Are You?" be as upset by the Protestant*

girl friend of his son as is the father in "Protestants Cry, Too?" I don't think so, or, at least, the tone of the story suggests he wouldn't be.

Tone is probably the operative word here. I sought to give the story a more ethnic feeling than the other story, made Frenchtown a more self-enclosed area with invisible but powerful walls separating it from the rest of the city. But focus and emphasis also play their roles.

In "Protestants Cry, Too" the emphasis is on Armand's love for a girl from the North Side. The love affair and the reaction of Armand's father allowed me to explore prejudice and the possibility of love—or compassion—overcoming it.

In "President Cleveland, Where Are You?" Armand is again in love with a girl from the other side of town, but this time the focus is on Jerry, the narrator, who discovers something in himself he had not recognized before.

In one story, Jerry is simply the narrator, the device through which the story is told. In the other, Jerry, still the narrator, is the crucial character to whom things happen. But Armand's involvement with a girl alien to Frenchtown is the wheel that turns both stories.

Thus, we have the same ingredients in both stories, the same basic situation and the same cast of characters, but the two stories are altogether different in tone and theme and plot.

# Protestants Cry, Too 🌿

To begin with, my brother Armand fell in love eleven times between Easter Sunday and Thanksgiving Day of 1938, and so it was no surprise, to me at least, when he announced at supper one night three years later that he wanted my parents' permission to marry.

After all, marriage seemed to be the inevitable destination of love, and I marvelled that he had not married long before.

My father took the news without expression, his doorway-wide shoulders hunched over the table as he chewed the blood sausage slowly and deliberately, but my mother flushed deeply, paled, looked at my father in horror and back at Armand in disbelief. My other brothers and sisters immediately set up a chorus of hoots and whistles, like a fleet of ships docking at Boston Harbor.

"But you're only nineteen," my mother protested, automatically passing the bowl of mashed potatoes to Esther. Her appetite shamed my mother but was a thing of pride to my father, who believed that an enormous quantity of food was as important to children as an enormous quantity of beer was to men.

"Well, if I'm old enough to work, I'm old enough to get married," Armand answered, addressing my mother defiantly while his eyes were sliding apprehensively to my father. Armand seldom looked uncertain. Hundreds of times I had seen him spear a line drive with finesse and send it arrowing to first base. He held the record for home runs with the Frenchtown Tigers and had broken more windows by his feats with the bat than any other boy in the neighborhood. In high school, Armand had been—of all things—the star of the Debating Team *(Resolved:* That the government should assume control of the nation's railroads) and he had also played basketball. And somehow he always found time for love.

"That's what makes the world go round, Jerry-boy," he'd tell me as I watched him combing his hair prior to a date.

I was much younger than Armand and had my private thoughts about love: foolish and unnecessarily troublesome, involving going to terrible dances and wearing Sunday clothes on, say, a Wednesday night and taking baths two or three times a week. Yet, I had to admit that if Armand pursued love so faithfully, certainly there must be some good in it.

At the supper table that night, however, I did not envy him and I suddenly realized that he had gradually changed in the past few months. He had been vague about the nature of his dates and he had been alternately happy and morose. Sometimes, he sat on the piazza steps in the evening, staring at nothing in particular and would dismiss me with a curt shake of his head when I asked him if he wanted to toss the baseball around for a while or bat me a few balls.

"How much are you making at the shop?" my father asked, reaching for another slice of bread.

"Fifty cents an hour and I'm due for a raise next month," Armand answered.

"How much have you saved?"

"Two hundred and ten dollars. And she's got almost as much. She's a secretary uptown and says she doesn't mind working to help us get settled."

"She . . . she," my mother said, exasperated. "Who is this *she?*"

"Yes, which one?" Esther asked. Her appetite apparently had been dealt a fatal blow by the announcement because she had put down her fork although her plate was still half full. "Is it Yolande or Theresa or Marie-Rose or Jeanne?"

My mother silenced her with a look.

"I thought you said there was safety in numbers, Ma," Paul offered. Paul was the smart one, a high honor student with a memory so acute that he got on your nerves.

"Enough," my father commanded like an umpire calling strike three. He turned to Armand. "My son, you're no longer a boy. You've been working more than a year since your graduation from high school. You've found out what it means to earn a living. And I admit that a man needs love and marriage and children."

My mother snorted with disgust. She always claimed that my father was incurably romantic, and she dreaded wedding receptions and anniversary parties at St. Jean's Hall because he always got sentimental and maudlin and drank too much beer and insisted on proposing innumerable toasts to the glories of love or singing old Canadian ballads about people dying of broken hearts.

"Would it be too much to tell us the name of this girl who is coming into the family?" my mother asked.

Armand scratched his head and tugged at his ear: a bad sign.

"Jessica Stone," he said.

"Jessica?" Esther asked. "What kind of name is that?"

"Stone . . . Stone," my mother mused.

"A Protestant," Paul exclaimed, his voice like a door slamming shut.

My mother made the sign of the cross, and in the awesome silence that followed we turned our eyes to my father. His head was bowed and his huge shoulders sagged in defeat. His knuckles were white where his hands gripped the table. I too clutched the table, tensing myself for the explosion to come. But when my father raised his head at last, there was no violence in his manner, although his voice filled me with fear because it was terrible in its quietness.

"All right," he said wearily. "You don't want a good Canadian girl, fine. Maybe you don't like pea soup. And an Irisher, fine, maybe you don't like corn beef and cabbage. And an Eye-talian, that, too, is all right if you don't like spaghetti." Fury gathered in his eyes. "But a Protestant? Are you crazy, my boy? Is that what we sent you to the good Catholic schools for? Is this what you were an altar boy for? To marry a Protestant?"

"I love her," Armand said, leaping to his feet. "This isn't Canada, Pa. This is the United States of America, 1941 . . ."

"Armand, Armand," my mother whispered, a pleading in her voice.

"Hey, Armand," Paul said, bright and interested. "What kind of Protestant?"

"What do you mean—what kind?" my father roared.

"Congregational," Armand said. "She sings in the choir at the Congregational Church. She's a good girl. She believes in God . . ."

Excitement danced in my veins. I had never known a Protestant. My family had come late from Canada and we had settled in a neighborhood far removed from the world of Protestants and Yankees. Although my father had become a fierce patriot, a staunch supporter of Franklin D. Roosevelt and a loyal Democrat, he seldom ventured outside of Frenchtown. As a result, I knew little of Protestants. They were people who lived on the other side of town, people who did not have to go to church on Sunday morning if they felt like staying in bed and whose churches closed up in the summer for vacations. Sister Angela assured us that Protestants could get to heaven, but she implied that this was allowed by the Catholic Church out of the goodness of its heart. Suddenly, my excitement fled by a sudden sense that the world was crumbling at my feet. My loyalty moved toward my father and mother, although I still ached for Armand, who stood at the table like some lonely hero who finds his deeds stricken from the rolls of honor.

My father suddenly relaxed. He shrugged and smiled. "Well, why should we get excited?" he asked my mother. "This week a Protestant and next week maybe a . . . a Hindu. And the week after that . . ."

"Next week and next year and forever, it will still be Jessica," Armand cried. "This isn't puppy love, Pa. I've been going out with her for seven months."

For Armand, of course, this was some sort or record.

"Seven months?" my father asked, astounded. "You've been going around with a Protestant for seven months behind my back?"

"Not behind your back," Armand said. "Have I ever brought any girl home here? No. Because I wanted to wait until I met the right one. And Jessica's the right one . . ."

"Well, don't plan on bringing *her* here," my father said. "I don't want her name mentioned again under this roof." He banged his fist on the table and a dish fell to the floor.

My mother jumped up in alarm, and Armand turned on his heel and left the house, slamming the door behind him.

So began what my brother Paul described as the Six-month War of the Renault family, and the war usually was fought at the supper table. My father was not a man for stiff rules, but he had always insisted that the entire family be home for supper, to break bread together at least once a day. Even Armand in his rebellion dared not break that law. Otherwise, however, he became a silent and brooding figure, spending little time at home. He worked all day in the comb shop and went off to meet his Jessica every evening. He didn't whistle off-key anymore as he dressed for his dates, and he acted as though we had all become invisible to him.

I had been pressed into service as a pitcher for the Tigers because Roger Lussier broke his arm, and I lost three games in a row. Armand agreed to give me some pointers, but he was not much help because he seemed like someone split in half, part of him murmuring to me, "Fine, fine," even when I threw a bad pitch, and another part of him far away, deep in thought. Paul said that a kind of doom hung over our house. He was melodramatic and often used words like *doom* and *holocaust* (Edgar Allan Poe was his favorite writer), and yet I had to admit that Armand's troubles had cast a shadow over us all.

Supper time became exercises in agony.

"I see in the paper where a fellow who left his religion got killed in a car crash in Boston," my father would offer to no one in particular.

"I'm not leaving my religion," Armand would reply, addressing the picture of the St. Lawrence River on the wall. "She's willing to take religious instruction, to go halfway . . ."

"Pass the gravy," my father would say.

And my mother would pass the gravy to my father while she looked with stricken eyes at Armand.

Or, my father would announce:

"I understand that the Blanchemaisons are going to lose their house. To the bank. A big-shot Protestant there is signing the papers tomorrow."

"Mister Blanchemaison has been drunk for six months and his family's on relief. It's the city that's making the bank take the house," Armand explained, looking at me as if I had brought up the question.

"And who's the mayor of the city? A Protestant, that's who," my father announced triumphantly to Esther, who looked at him in perplexity.

Or, with a quiet air of victory, he would ask my mother, "You know Theophile LeBlanc, the caterer? Well, he was putting on a feed at a fancy Protestant wedding last Saturday. He said that it was disgusting. Nobody sang any songs, nobody danced and nobody even got drunk. They stood around and ate sandwiches made with crackers. People who don't sing and dance at a wedding: they don't have hearts . . ."

One day I burst into the house after finally winning a ball game (although I almost spoiled the victory by giving up four home runs in the ninth inning) and found the rooms unusually quiet, all the kids gone off somewhere, and my father at work. I heard voices in the parlor and was about to enter when I halted in my tracks, held back by the intimate quality of the voices.

"I know, I know, Armand," my mother was saying. "I agree that she's a nice girl. Polite and charming. But going behind your father's back to meet her is one thing—inviting her here, without warning him, is another . . ."

"But don't you see, Ma," Armand said, "that he thinks all Protestants are some kind of monsters because he's never really known one? I'll bet he's never spoken more than five minutes with a Protestant. You met Jessica. You say she's a fine girl. I think Pa will, too, if he has a chance to meet her . . ."

"I still get the shivers wondering what he'll say when he learns that I've met her, that we sat in a drugstore together and had a college ice . . ."

"Please, Ma," Armand pleaded. "His bark is worse than his bite. You always said he's a sentimental man."

"I don't know, Armand, I don't know," she said, her voice tender and troubled.

I drew back in horror, appalled at the conspiracy, my mother's treachery, her disloyalty to my father. I ran up the street to meet him; and as I saw him stalking home from work, I became aware for the first time of my father as a *person*, not simply a big man who either roared with anger or boomed with laughter, who consumed incredible amounts of beer and whose word was law. Knowing that he could be betrayed gave him a sudden, human countenance. I studied the deep lines on his face, the network of wrinkles near his eyes that had always fascinated me because of their resemblance to spider webs, and I realized that they were the result of long hard days at work and the problems of bringing up a family. And instead of bursting out my information, I remained silent and carried his empty lunchpail, shy with him suddenly and warm and itchy all over my body.

The following Sunday afternoon, I cried out in astonishment as I glanced out the parlor window and saw Armand coming along the sidewalk with a girl. He held her elbow tenderly, as if she were fragile and precious beyond price.

He didn't look where he was going but gazed at her raptly. I had to admit that I did not blame him for staring at her: she was slender and blond and lovely, dressed in something pink and white, and the colors blended with the soft tones of her delicate face. The autumn wind rose suddenly and she lifted her hand to hold a tiny pink hat, the gesture filled with grace. I myself would have gladly run a mile to chase that hat for her if the wind chanced to blow it off.

My mother stood beside me, her cheeks flushed, her eyes wide with concern. She looked like the guilty party who is unmasked in the last chapter of the serials at the Globe Theater on Saturday afternoons.

"God help us," she whispered breathlessly. Straightening her shoulders and sighing, she called to my father: "Louis, company's coming up the street . . ."

My father, who was in the kitchen listening to the Red Sox baseball game on the radio, groaned loudly. "Company? Who comes to disturb a man after dinner on Sunday?" My father pretended that he wanted only privacy on weekends or in the evenings, but when company did arrive he played the role of the perfect host to the hilt, keeping the beer flowing and my mother busy serving food. People usually found it hard to leave because my father always insisted on one more drink, one more joke, one more argument.

My mother greeted Armand and Jessica at the front door as my father entered the living room, yawning and straightening his tie. Armand's entrance caught him with his mouth wide open. My father jerked his tie, his mouth closed in surprise and he stood rigidly in the doorway.

The scent of a subtle perfume filled the air as the girl entered. Her eyes were blue, and for the first time I realized that blue was the most beautiful color in the world.

"This is Jessica Stone," Armand announced, his hand still at her elbow but protectively now. "Jessica, this is my father and mother." I had to suppress a giggle at his formality. "And my brother Jerry," he added, pointing to me. "The other kids are out somewhere, playing around."

Jessica smiled hesitantly and I saw her hand tremble at her side. Armand guided her to the davenport. I wondered whether her cheeks gave her pain: that smile seemed to be hurting her. And no wonder, I thought, as I looked at my father, who stood like a figure of wrath at the doorway.

My mother seemed to be everywhere at once, adjusting the curtain, flicking an invisible speck of dust from the end table, touching Armand's shoulder and pushing me from the room. I heard the big leather chair squeak menacingly as my father lowered himself into it.

Shamelessly, I stood near the door, straining to catch every sound and nuance of the conversation. My mother and Armand carried on a strange wandering conversation about the weather, talking at length of tumbling leaves and the great amount of rain that had fallen during the week and the way nights were becoming chilly. I was impatient for the foolish conversation to end. Finally, a huge silence settled in the room.

Roger Lussier called to me from the outside steps, and I remembered in dismay that we were supposed to go to the movies. I didn't answer, hoping he would go away.

After a while, my father cleared his throat. "I was listening to the ball game," he said. "Do you follow baseball?"

I peeked into the room and saw Jessica sitting stiffly beside Armand. "I play tennis," she said.

"Tennis," my father said, as if that were the most ridiculous sport in the world.

"She's very good," Armand offered. "She won a trophy last year."

Silence again except for Roger's voice, sounding impatient and shrill now.

"Your father. Where does he work?" my father asked.

"In the Savings Bank," she answered.

"A banker?" my father inquired, giving the word the same contempt that he used for Republican.

"He's a teller," she amended.

"But he works in a bank," my father declared, with a kind of triumph.

"Yes," she answered, her voice strained.

Roger was setting up such a howl outside that I went to the back door. Actually, I was somewhat relieved to end my eavesdropping because I shared the pain and embarrassment of Jessica Stone. Roger was worried that we would be late for the movie, but my mind was still in the parlor.

"All right," I told him. "Let's go. But wait just one minute more . . ." I reentered the house and stood by the parlor doorway again.

"Franklin D. Roosevelt is the greatest president the country ever had," my father was saying. "The greatest man in the world."

"Abraham Lincoln was a great president, too," Jessica answered, a hint of defiance in her voice.

I couldn't bear to listen any further and was happy to join Roger on the back steps. I was in a hurry to get to the Globe Theater, or any place that was far away from the inquisition going on in the parlor.

When I arrived home at supper time, my father was sitting in the kitchen, exuding an air of victory. His shoes were off and his feet extended luxuriously out on the floor. My mother busied herself at the stove: there was always something cooking there, morning, noon and night, that needed her attention.

"And did you see her sitting there so prim and proper?" my father was asking. "What kind of girl is that? I tell you, it's like Theophile LeBlanc said. Protestants have no juices. Did you see the girl smile? No. Did she laugh? No. And anyone who thinks that Abraham Lincoln is greater than Franklin D. Roosevelt . . ." He shook his head in disbelief.

"Louis . . . Louis," my mother said. "She's a nice girl, a fine girl, and she loves your son. Does it matter what she thinks of Roosevelt or Lincoln? Does it matter what church she goes to?" A bit of anger crept into her voice. "And how could you act so rude to a guest in your house?"

"But don't you see?" he asked. "I wanted to show Armand that the girl is not for him, that she would not fit into his life, into our life. She plays tennis. She doesn't follow the Red Sox. She sings in a Protestant choir. And it's plain to see she's a Republican . . ."

"But she's hardly old enough to vote," my mother said.

"Well, maybe we'll see a change in Armand now," my father said, settling back, wriggling his feet, "now that I've"—he groped for the word and pinned it down exultantly—"*exposed* her."

My father's exposure of Jessica Stone did not affect Armand's love for her. In fact, he announced a few nights later that he was planning to give her an engagement ring for Christmas. My father closed his eyes when he heard the news and his lips moved in what I hoped was a silent prayer but feared was an oath too terrible for us to hear. I looked at my father and Armand and my mother and did some praying of my own. I felt allegiance to my father whose oldest son was defying him, who was ready to turn his back on his family and who no longer was interested in such things as baseball for the sake of a girl. Yet, I also sympathized with Armand because I agreed that Jessica Stone was more beautiful than any girl in Frenchtown. And my heart also had room for my mother, torn between her husband and her son. When I saw the sorrow in her face as she looked at one and then the other, I easily forgave her for going behind my father's back to help Armand. And yet . . . yet, I was tired of the situation because it seemed to me that there were more important things in the world than love, and everytime I brought up one of these things—for instance, the frustrating December weather that had not turned cold enough for ice skating—someone would tell me to go out and play or Paul would accuse me of having no appreciation of drama. I wanted to tell him that if drama was something that made your chest ache with strangeness, then I wanted no part of it.

We were all involved in a large drama, however, when the voice of the announcer on the radio one Sunday afternoon stunned us with the news that the Japanese had attacked a place called Pearl Harbor.

My father jumped from his chair in alarm and excitement, indignant to learn that someone had dared challenge the nation led by Franklin D. Roosevelt.

"Paul," he bellowed. "Paul . . ."

My brother came running from the bedroom where he had been reading a book as usual.

"Where is Pearl Harbor?" my father asked him.

"In Hawaii," Paul answered promptly.

We learned more about Pearl Harbor and the vast world of the Pacific Ocean in the weeks to come, and my father spent many hours at the radio, shaking his head at the news, perpetually angry. He seemed to take it as a personal insult that American boys were being wounded and dying.

One supper time when my father, after the usual prayer of grace, added another prayer for the good American boys who were in battle, Armand said: "A good many of those boys are Protestants . . ."

My father paused, deep in thought. "And a good many are Catholic, too," he answered after a while, the belligerency gone from his voice.

"Well, here's one Catholic you can add to the roll. I'm going to enlist."

A sharp cry came from my mother, but somehow I had eyes only for my father. For the first time in months, he looked at Armand directly.

"No," my father protested. "You're just a boy . . ."

"I'm an American," Armand said.

"I thought you were going to get married in the spring," Paul interjected.

"Jessica and I talked it over," Armand said. "How can we get married when there's a war going on? She said she's willing to wait . . ." He looked at my father. "Pa, I want your permission to enlist. Me and Jessica, that's something else. I know you don't approve of us, but I'll tell you this much: as soon as I come back, we're going to be married."

"But why volunteer?" my father asked. "There are a lot of others who can go."

His question surprised me because it was obvious that Armand's enlistment would solve the problem of his romance. I pondered again the mysterious ways of grown-ups. For myself, I had no fear for Armand's safety. In my eyes, he had been born to become a hero, whether on a baseball field or in battle, and I was sure of his indestructibility.

"Every man has his duty to perform," Armand said, and his words were quiet and somehow sad and gallant.

Incredibly, tears formed in the corners of my father's eyes. At first, I thought he must be sick because I had never seen him cry before. He sniffed and blew his nose and cleared his throat.

"Hey, Pa," Paul said. "You're crying."

"Who's crying?" my father bellowed, his wet eyes finding my mother, who sat stunned and grief-stricken across from him, her face cruelly bleak as if winter had blown across her features. "It's the onions in the soup," my father said. "Onions always bring tears to a man's eyes . . ."

The clock in the steeple of the Congregational Church in the square stroked the hour of nine and we listened to its echoes in the crisp morning air. The army bus stood at the corner and I was fascinated by its color, the olive drab giving an air of emergency to the gathering of people on the sidewalk. The fellows who were leaving for military service were not yet in uniform, but already there was a hint of the military in their bearing. A soldier in uniform paced the sidewalk impatiently near the bus.

My father and I stood with Armand in front of King's Shoe Store. My mother had remained at home, having kissed Armand goodbye without allowing tears to fall, and unwilling to take the chance of breaking down as he got on the bus. The other children were in school, but my father had allowed me to see Armand off.

"I hope they send us down South for basic training," Armand said. "At least, it'll be warm there." His voice seemed unnaturally thin and high-pitched, and his eyes searched the square, looking for Jessica. I saw her first, the blond hair vivid in the drabness of the morning. She walked swiftly toward us, opening her arms to Armand as she approached, but she arrested the gesture when she saw my father. They had not met since that terrible Sunday in the parlor.

My father shifted on one foot and then another. Finally, he looked down at me. "Come, Jerry, let's go find that soldier and ask him when the bus is leaving . . ."

"Thanks, Pa," Armand said.

As we approached the soldier, he placed a silver whistle in his mouth and blew it fiercely. He called out: "Okay, you guys, fall in. On the double. On the double . . ." He would have made a fine cheerleader.

My father and I returned to Armand and Jessica, who were holding hands, huddled together as if the day had suddenly turned too cold to bear.

"It's time," my father said, touching Armand's shoulder.

Armand drew back his shoulders and shook hands with my father. He punched me lightly on the arm. He turned to Jessica and kissed her gently on the cheek and then gathered her in his arms, holding her closely. He pulled away from her abruptly and looked at us all for a long moment, his face pale and his chin trembling a little. And then he walked quickly toward the bus and was lost in the crowd of fellows who were leaving with him.

Jessica turned away from us. She kept her face averted as the bus gradually filled, as the soldier took one final look around the square, as the motor roared into life. Armand waved to us from inside the bus, but there was little comfort in that last glimpse.

The bus turned the corner and was gone. The people began to disperse and my father, Jessica, and I seemed to be alone as if we were standing on a small invisible island there in the square. She still did not look at us, although I could see the reflection of her face in a store window. Clutching her coat at the neck, she left us abruptly, walking away without warning.

My father watched her go, shrugging his shoulders.

"Pa," I said, "you were wrong."

"What do you mean, wrong?" he asked gruffly, pulling his handkerchief out of his pocket.

"You said Protestants have no heart, that they don't laugh or cry. Jessica was crying. I saw her face and she was crying just like you cried the other night at supper."

He looked at her retreating figure. He blew his nose feebly and the sound was not as magnificent as usual, barely audible above the traffic. He lifted his arms and let them drop at his sides.

"There's no fool like an old fool," he said, mysteriously. Then: "Come, Jerry, let's go find her before she's too far away . . ."

I had to run to keep pace with him as we threaded our way through the crowd. We finally caught up to her near the drinking fountain on the other side of the square. My father touched her arm, and suddenly she was folded in his embrace and never before had I seen people look so happy while they were crying.

# Guess What? I Almost Kissed My Father Goodnight ✀

# Introduction 🌿

*I* left the newspaper earlier than usual that particular afternoon, for a reason I have now forgotten. Driving through the downtown area, I remembered an errand that had to be run. Which meant I would have to turn around, drive across town, find a parking space, and so forth. I drew the car up at the curb, pausing there, letting the traffic flow by, wondering whether the errand was worth the bother.

"Dad!"

I turned at the voice. My son, Peter, then in high school, was regarding me with surprise.

"What are you doing here?" he asked.

I explained. "And what are you doing here?"

He told me that school had ended early because of a teachers' conference. He looked at me curiously as he got into the car. I felt his eyes on me as I drove. Once, glancing at him, I was startled to see something that resembled suspicion in his eyes. Why? Then I realized he had suddenly seen me out of context, in a car downtown in the middle of the day, not at home, not at work. We drove along without further comment.

A small moment in an ordinary day. But that meeting turned out to contain the seeds of "Guess What? I Almost Kissed My Father Goodnight."

*Fathers are mysterious beings to their children. At least, my father was to me. Which is strange because he was an ordinary man. He worked in a factory eight hours a day, five days a week. He loved the Boston Red Sox despite their inability to win a pennant most years. He enjoyed cold beer at the end of the day. He was affectionate with his wife and children, never left the house or returned without a kiss for my mother. As I grew older, we became friends. But there were certain things I couldn't ask him. What did he think about as he sat at the bench eight hours a day? What dreams and hopes wafted him to sleep as he took a nap after supper? Was he disappointed with his life? Or had he found fulfillment? I knew so much about him—from his shoe size (6½ or 7, depending on the style) to his favorite singer (Bing Crosby), but there was so much that I would never know.*

*That downtown encounter with Peter caused me to wonder whether he might feel the same way. He had always seen me in the familiar role of father—but did that sudden meeting make him regard me for once as an individual, a person distinct from the father figure I had always been? And what if . . .*

*There it was again, that perennial question.*

*I embarked on a story in which the narrator is a sixteen-year-old boy who "investigates" his father, who learns his shoe and shirt sizes and a lot of other things, although he is searching for something altogether different. The story is told from the boy's viewpoint because I wanted to preserve the mystery of the father, to show that although some questions are never really answered, there are tantalizing hints and indications.*

*Years later, long after the story had been written and appeared in print, I asked Peter if he remembered that midday meeting on Main Street.*

*He thought a moment. "Vaguely," he said.*

*But I don't think he remembered at all.*

*Which is, perhaps, another story.*

# Guess What?
## I Almost Kissed
## My Father
## Goodnight 🌱

**I**'ve got to get to the bottom of it all somehow and maybe this is the best way. It's about my father. For instance, I found out recently that my father is actually forty-five years old. I knew that he was forty-something but it never meant anything to me. I mean, trying to imagine someone over forty and what it's like to be that old is the same as trying to imagine what the world would be like in, say, 1999. Anyway, he's forty-five, and he has the kind of terrible job that fathers have; in his case, he's office manager for a computer equipment concern. Nine-to-five stuff. Four weeks vacation every year but two weeks must be taken between January and May so he usually ends up painting the house or building a patio or something like that in April, and then we travel the other two weeks in July. See America First. He reads a couple of newspapers every day and never misses the seven o'clock news on television.

Here are some other vital statistics my research turned up: He's five ten, weighs 160 pounds, has a tendency toward high blood pressure, enjoys a glass of beer or two while he's watching the Red Sox on television, sips one martini and never two before dinner, likes his steak medium rare and has a habit of saying that "tonight, by God, I'm going to stay up and watch Johnny Carson," but always gropes his way to bed after the eleven o'clock news, which he watches only to learn the next day's weather forecast. He has a pretty good sense of humor but a weakness for awful puns which he inflicts on us at the dinner table: "Do you carrot all for me? I'm in a stew over you." We humor him. By we, I mean my sisters. Annie, who is nineteen and away at college, and Debbie, who is fourteen and spends her life on the telephone. And me: I'm Mike, almost sixteen and a sophomore in high school. My mother's name is Ellen— Dad calls her Ellie—and she's a standard mother: "Clean up your room! Is your homework done?"

Now that you've gotten the basic details, I'll tell you about that day last month when I walked downtown from school to connect with the North Side bus which deposits me in front of my house. It was one of those terrific days in spring and the air smelled like vacation, and it made you ache with all the things you wanted to do and all the places you wanted to see and all the girls you wanted to meet. Like the girl at the bus stop that I've been trying to summon up the nerve to approach for weeks: so beautiful she turns my knees liquid. Anyway, I barreled through Bryant Park, a shortcut, the turf spring-soft and spongy under my feet and the weeping willows hazy with blossom. Suddenly I screeched to a halt, like Bugs Bunny in one of those crazy television cartoons. There's a car parked near the Civil War cannon. Ours. I recognize the dent in the right front fender Annie put there last month when she was home from college. And there are also those decals on the side window that give the geography of our boring vacation trips, *Windy Chasms*, places like that.

The car is unoccupied. Did somebody steal it and abandon it here? Wow, great! I walk past the splashing fountain that displays one of those embarrassing naked cherubs and stop short again. There he is: my father. Sitting on a park bench. Gazing out over a small pond that used to have goldfish swimming around until kids started stealing them. My father was deep in thought, like a statue in a museum. I looked at my watch. Two-thirty in the afternoon, for crying out loud. What was he doing there at this time of day? I was about to approach him but hesitated, held back for some reason—I don't know why. Although he looked perfectly normal, I felt as though I had somehow caught him naked, had trespassed on forbidden territory, the way I'm afraid to have my mother come barging into my bedroom at certain moments. I drew back, studying him as if he were a sudden stranger. I saw the familiar thinning short hair, the white of his scalp showing through. The way the flesh in his neck has begun to pucker like turkey skin. Now, he sighed. I saw his shoulders heave, and the rest of his body shudder like the chain reaction of freight cars. He lifted his face to the sun, eyes closed. He seemed to be reveling in the moment, all his pores open. I tiptoed away. People talk about tiptoeing but I don't think I ever really tiptoed before in my life. Anyway, I leave him there, still basking on that park bench, because I've got something more important to do at the bus stop. Today, I have vowed to approach the girl, talk to her, say something, *anything*. After all, I'm not exactly Frankenstein and some girls actually think I'm fun to be with. Anyway, she isn't at the bus stop. I stall around and miss the two-forty-five deliberately. She never shows up. At three-thirty, I thumb home and pick up a ride in a green MG, which kind of compensates for a rotten afternoon.

At dinner that evening, I'm uncommunicative, thinking of the girl and all the science homework waiting in my room. Dinner at our house is a kind of ritual that alternates between bedlam and boredom with no sense of direction whatever. Actually, I don't enjoy table talk. I have this truly tremendous appetite and I eat too fast, like my mother says. The trouble is that I'm always being asked a question or expected to laugh at some corny joke when my mouth is full, which it usually is. But that evening I stopped eating altogether when my mother asked my father about his day at the office.

"Routine," he said.

I thought of that scene in the park.

"Did you have to wait around all day for that Harper contract?" my mother asked.

"Didn't even have time for a coffee break," he said, reaching for more potatoes.

I almost choked on the roast beef. He lied: my father actually lied. I sat there, terrified, caught in some kind of terrible no-man's-land. It was as if the lie itself had thrust me into panic. Didn't I fake my way through life most of the time—telling half-truths to keep everybody happy, either my parents or my teachers or even my friends? What would happen if everybody started telling the truth all of a sudden? But I was bothered by his motive. I mean—why did he have to pretend that he *wasn't* in the park that afternoon? And that first question came back to haunt me worse than before—what was he doing there, anyway, in the first place?

I found myself studying him across the table, scrutinizing him with the eyes of a stranger. But it didn't work. He was simply my father. Looked exactly as he always did. He was his usual dull unruffled self, getting ready to take his evening nap prior to the television news. Stifling a yawn after dessert. Forget it, I told myself. There's a simple explanation for everything.

Let's skip some time now until the night of the telephone call. And let me explain about the telephone setup at our house. First of all, my father never answers the phone. He lets it ring nine or ten or eleven times and merely keeps on reading the paper and watching television because he claims—and he's right—that most of the calls are for Debbie or me. Anyway, a few nights after that happening at the park, the phone rang about ten-thirty and I barreled out of my room because he and my mother get positively explosive about calls after nine on school nights.

When I lifted the receiver, I found that my father had already picked up the downstairs extension. There was a pause and then he said: "I've got it, Mike."

"Yes, sir," I said. And hung up.

I stood there in the upstairs hallway, not breathing. His voice was a murmur and even at that distance I detected some kind of intimacy. Or did the distance itself contribute that hushed, secretive quality? I returned to my room and put a Blood, Sweat and Tears on the stereo. I remembered that my mother was out for the evening, a meeting of the Ladies' Auxiliary. I got up and looked in the mirror. Another lousy pimple, on the right side of my nose to balance the one on the left. Who had called him on the telephone at that hour of the night? And why had he answered the call in record time? Was it the same person he'd been waiting for in Bryant Park? Don't be ridiculous, Mike, I told myself; think of real stuff, like pimples. Later, I went downstairs and my father was slumped in his chair, newspaper like a fragile tent covering his face. His snores capsized the tent and it slid to the floor. He needed a shave, his beard like small slivers of ice. His feet were fragile, something I had never noticed before; they were mackerel white, half in and half out of his slippers. I went back upstairs without checking the refrigerator, my hunger suddenly annihilated by guilt. He wasn't mysterious: he was my father. And he snored with his mouth open.

The next day I learned the identity of the girl at the bus stop: like a bomb detonating. Sally Bettencourt. There's a Sally Bettencourt in every high school in the world—the girl friend of football heroes, the queen of the prom, Miss Apple Blossom Time. That's Sally Bettencourt of Monument High. And I'm not a football hero, although I scored three points in the intramural basketball tournament last winter. And she *did* smile at me a few weeks ago while waiting for the bus. Just for the record, let me put down here how I found out her name. She was standing a few feet from me, chatting with some girls and fellows, and I drifted toward her and saw her name written on the cover of one of her books. Detective work.

The same kind of detective work sent me investigating my father's desk the next day. He keeps all his private correspondence and office papers in an old battered roll-top my mother found at an auction and sandpapered and refinished. No one was at home. The desk was unlocked. I opened drawers and checked some diary-like type note-books. Nothing but business stuff. All kinds of receipts. Stubs of cancelled checks. Dull. But a bottom drawer revealed the kind of box that contains correspondence paper and envelopes. Inside, I found envelopes of different shapes and sizes and colors. Father's Day cards he had saved through the years. I found one with a scrawled "Mikey" painstakingly written when I was four or five probably. His secret love letters—from Annie and Debbie and me.

"Looking for something?"

His shadow fell across the desk. I mumbled something, letting irritation show in my voice. I have found that you can fake adults out by muttering and grumbling as if you're using some foreign language that they couldn't possibly understand. And they feel intimidated or confused. Anyway, they decide not to challenge you or make an issue of it. That's what happened at that moment. There I was snooping in my father's desk and because I muttered unintelligibly when he interrupted me, *he* looked embarrassed while I stalked from the room as if I was the injured party, ready to bring suit in court.

Three things happened in the next week and they had nothing to do with my father: First, I called Sally Bettencourt. The reason why I called her is that I could have sworn she smiled again at me at the bus stop one afternoon. I mean, not a polite smile but a smile for *me*, as if she recognized me as a person, an individual. Actually I called her three times in four days. She was *(a)* not at home and the person on the line (her mother? her sister?) had no idea when she'd arrive; *(b)* she was taking a shower—"Any message?" "No"; *(c)* the line was busy. What would I have said to her, if she'd answered? I've always had the feeling that I'm a real killer on the phone when I don't have to worry about what to do with my hands or how bad my posture is. The second thing that happened was a terrible history test which I almost flunked: a low C that could possibly keep me off the Honor Roll, which would send my mother into hysterics. Number 3: I received my assignment from the Municipal Park Department for my summer job—lifeguard at Pool Number 38. Translation: Pool Number 38 is for children twelve years old and younger, not the most romantic pool in the city.

Bugged by history, I talked Mister Rogers, the teacher, into allowing me some extra work to rescue my mark and I stayed up late one night, my stereo earphones clamped on my head so that I wouldn't disturb anyone as the cool sounds of the Tinted Orange poured into my ears. Suddenly, I awoke—shot out of a cannon. My watch said one-twenty. One-twenty in the morning. I yawned. My mouth felt rotten, as if the French Foreign Legion had marched through it barefoot (one of my father's old jokes that I'd heard about a million times). I went downstairs for a glass of orange juice. A light spilled from the den. I sloshed orange juice on my shirt as I stumbled toward the room. He's there: my father. Slumped in his chair. Like death. And I almost drop dead myself. But his lips flutter and he produces an enormous snore. One arm dangles to the floor, limp as a draped towel. His fingers are almost touching a book that had evidently fallen from his hand. I pick it up. Poetry. A poet I never heard of. Kenneth Fearing. Riffling the pages, I find that the poems are mostly about the Depression. In the front of the book there's an inscription. Delicate handwriting, faded lavender ink. "To Jimmy, I'll never forget you. Muriel." Jimmy? My father's name is James and my mother and his friends call him Jim. But Jimmy? I notice a date at the bottom of the page, meticulously recorded in that same fragile handwriting— November 2, 1942—when he was young enough to be called Jimmy. By some girl whose name was Muriel, who gave him a book of poems that he takes out and reads in the dead of night even if they are poems about the Depression. He stirs, grunting, clearing his throat, his hand like a big white spider searching the floor for the book. I replace the book on the floor and glide out of the room and back upstairs.

The next day I began my investigation in earnest and overlooked no details. That's when I found out what size shoes, socks, shirts, etc., that he wears. I looked in closets and bureaus, his workbench in the cellar, not knowing what I was searching for but the search itself important. There was one compensation: at least, it kept my mind off Sally Bettencourt. I had finally managed to talk to her on the telephone. We spoke mostly in monosyllables. It took me about ten minutes to identify myself ("The fellow at *what* bus stop?") because apparently all those smiles sent in my direction had been meaningless and my face was as impersonal as a label on a can of soup. The conversation proceeded downward from that point and reached bottom when she said: "Well, thanks for calling, Mark." I didn't bother to correct her. She was so sweet about it all. All the Sally Bettencourts of the world are that way: that's why you keep on being in love with them when you know it's entirely useless. Even when you hang up and see your face in the hallway mirror—what a terrible place to hang a mirror— your face all crumpled up like a paper bag. And the following day, she wasn't at the bus stop, of course. But then neither was I.

What I mean about the bus stop is this: I stationed myself across the street to get a glimpse of her, to see if she really was as beautiful as I remembered or if the phone call had diminished her loveliness. When she didn't arrive, I wandered through the business district. Fellows and girls lingered in doorways. Couples held hands crossing the street. A record store blared out "Purple Evenings" by the Tinted Orange. I spotted my father. He was crossing the street, dodging traffic, as if he was dribbling an invisible ball down a basketball court. I checked my watch: two fifty-five. Stepping into a doorway, I observed him hurrying past the Merchants Bank and Appleton's Department Store and the Army-Navy Surplus Supply Agency. He paused in front of the Monument Public Library. And disappeared inside. My father—visiting the library? He didn't even have a library card, for crying out loud.

I'm not exactly crazy about libraries, either. Everybody whispers or talks low as if the building has a giant volume knob turned down to practically zero. As I stood there, I saw Laura Kincaid drive up in her new LeMans. A quiet, dark green LeMans. Class. "If I had to describe Laura Kincaid in one word, it would be 'class,' " I'd heard my father say once. The car drew into a parking space, as if the space had been waiting all day for her arrival. She stepped out of the door. She is blond, her hair the color of lemonade as it's being poured on a hot day. I stood there, paralyzed. A scene leaped in my mind: Laura Kincaid at a New Year's Party at our house, blowing a toy horn just before midnight while I watched in awe from the kitchen, amazed at how a few glasses of booze could convert all these bankers and Rotary Club members and Chamber of Commerce officials into the terrible kind of people you see dancing to Guy Lombardo on television while the camera keeps cutting back to Times Square where thousands of other people, most of them closer to my age, were also acting desperately happy. I stood there thinking of that stuff because I was doing some kind of juggling act in my mind—trying to figure out why was she at this moment walking across the street, heading for the library, her hair a lemon halo in the sun, her nylons flashing as she hurried. What was her hurry? There was barely any traffic. Was she on her way to a rendezvous? Stop it, you nut, I told myself, even as I made my way to the side entrance.

The library is three stories high, all the stacks and bookshelves built around an interior courtyard. I halted near the circulation desk with no books in my arms to check out. Feeling ridiculous, I made my way to the bubbler. The spray of water was stronger than I expected: my nostrils were engulfed by water. For some reason, I thought of Sally Bettencourt and how these ridiculous events kept happening to me and I ached with longing for her, a terrible emptiness inside of me that needed to be filled. I climbed the stairs to the third floor, my eyes flying all over the place, trying to spot my father. And Laura Kincaid. And knowing all the time that it was merely a game, impossible, ridiculous.

And then I saw them. Together. Standing at the entrance to the alcove that was marked 818 to 897. Two books were cradled in her arms like babies. My father wasn't looking at the books or the shelves or the walls or the ceilings or the floor or anything. He was looking at her. Then, they laughed. It was like a silent movie. I mean—I saw their eyes light up and their lips moving but didn't hear anything. My father shook his head, slowly, a smile lingering tenderly on his face. I drew back into the alcove labeled 453 to 521, across from them, apprehensive, afraid that suddenly they might see me spying on them. His hand reached up and touched her shoulder. They laughed again, still merrily. She indicated the books in her arms. He nodded, an eagerness in his manner. He didn't look as if he had ever snored in his life or taken a nap after dinner. They looked around. She glanced at her watch. He gestured vaguely.

Pressed against the metal bookshelf, I felt conspicuous, vulnerable, as if they would suddenly whirl and see me, and point accusing fingers. But nothing like that happened. She finally left, simply walked away, the books still in her arm. My father watched her go, his face in shadow. She walked along the balcony, then down the spiral stairs, the nylons still flashing, her hair a lemon waterfall. My father watched until she disappeared from view. I squinted, trying to discern his features, to see whether he was still my father, searching for the familiar landmarks of his face and body, needing some kind of verification. I watched him for a minute or two as he stood there looking down, his eyes tracing the path of her departure as if she were still visible. I studied his face: was this my father? And then this terrible numbness invaded my body, like a Novocaine of the spirit, killing all my emotions. And the numbness even pervaded my mind, slowing down my thoughts. For which I was grateful. All the way home on the bus, I stared out the window, looking at the landscapes and the buildings and the people but not really seeing them, as if I was storing them in my mind like film to develop them later when they'd have meaning for me.

At dinner, the food lay unappetizingly on my plate. I had to fake my way through the meal, lifting the fork mechanically. I found it difficult not to look at my father. What I mean is—I didn't want to look at him. And because I didn't, I kept doing it. Like when they tell you not to think of a certain subject and you can't help thinking of it.

"Aren't you feeling well, Mike?" my mother asked.

I leaped about five feet off my chair. I hadn't realized how obvious I must have appeared: the human eating machine suddenly toying with his food—steak, at that, which requires special concentration.

"He's probably in love," Debbie said.

And that word *love*. I found it difficult to keep my eyes away from my father.

"I met Laura Kincaid at the library today," I heard my father say.

"Was she able to get a copy of the play?" my mother asked.

"Two of them," he said, munching. "I still think *Streetcar Named Desire* is pretty ambitious for you girls to put on."

"The Women's Auxiliary knows no fear of Tennessee Williams," my mother said in that exaggerated voice she uses when she's kidding around.

"You know, that's funny, Dad," I heard myself saying. "I saw you in the library this afternoon and was wondering what you were doing there."

"Oh? I didn't see you, Mike."

"He was supposed to pick up the play on my library card. But then Laura Kincaid came by . . ." That was my mother explaining it all, although I barely made out the words.

I won't go into the rest of the scene and I won't say that my appetite suddenly came back and that I devoured the steak. Because I didn't. That was two days ago and I still feel funny about it all. Strange I mean. That's why I'm writing this, putting it all down, all the evidence I gathered. That first time in the park when he was sitting there. The telephone call. That book of poetry he reads late at night, "To Jimmy, I'll never forget you. Muriel." Laura Kincaid in the library. Not much evidence, really. Especially when I look at him and see how he's my father all right.

Last night, I came downstairs after finishing my homework and he had just turned off the television set. "Cloudy tomorrow, possible showers," he said, putting out the lights in the den.

We stood there in the half-darkness.

"Homework done, Mike?"

"Yes."

"Hey, Dad."

"Yes, Mike?" Yawning.

I didn't plan to ask him. But it popped out. "I was looking through a book of yours the other day. Poetry by some guy named Fearing or Nearing or something." I couldn't see his face in the half dark. Keeping my voice light, I said: "Who's this Muriel who gave you the book, anyway?"

His laugh was a playful bark. "Boy, that was a long time ago. Muriel Stanton." He closed the kitchen window. "I asked her to go the Senior Prom but she went with someone else. We were friends. I mean—I thought we were more than friends until she went to the Prom with someone else. And so she gave me a gift—of friendship—at graduation." We walked into the kitchen together. "That's a lousy swap, Mike. A book instead of a date with a girl you're crazy about." He smiled ruefully. "Hadn't thought of good old Muriel for years."

You see? Simple explanations for everything. And if I exposed myself as a madman and asked him about the other stuff, the park and the telephone call, I knew there would be perfectly logical reasons. And yet. And yet. I remember that day in the library, when Laura Kincaid walked away from him. I said that I couldn't see his face, not clearly anyway, but I could see a bit of his expression. And it looked familiar but I couldn't pin it down. And now I realized why it was familiar: it reminded me of my own face when I looked into the mirror the day I hung up the phone after talking to Sally Bettencourt. All kind of crumpled up. Or was that my imagination? Hadn't my father been all the way across the library courtyard, too far away for me to tell what kind of expression was on his face?

Last night, standing in the kitchen, as I poured a glass of milk and he said: "Doesn't your stomach ever get enough?" I asked him: "Hey, Dad. You get lonesome sometimes? I mean: that's a crazy question, maybe. But I figure grown-ups, like fathers and mothers—you get to feeling *down* sometimes, don't you?"

I could have sworn his eyes narrowed and something leaped in them, some spark, some secret thing that had suddenly come out of hiding.

"Sure, Mike. Everybody gets the blues now and then. Even fathers are people. Sometimes, I can't sleep and get up and sit in the dark in the middle of the night. And it gets lonesome because you think of . . ."

"What do you think of, Dad?"

He yawned. "Oh, a lot of things."

That's all. And here I am sitting up in the middle of the night writing this, feeling lonesome, thinking of Sally Bettencourt, and how I haven't a chance with her and thinking, too, of Muriel Stanton who wouldn't go to the Senior Prom with my father. How he gets lonesome sometimes. And sits up in the night, reading poetry. I think of his anguished face at the library and the afternoon at Bryant Park, and all the mysteries of his life that show he's a person. Human.

Earlier tonight, I saw him in his chair, reading the paper, and I said, "Goodnight, Dad," and he looked up and smiled, but an absent kind of smile, as if he was thinking of something else, long ago and far away, and, for some ridiculous feeling, I felt like kissing him goodnight. But didn't, of course. Who kisses his father at sixteen?

# My First Negro

# Introduction ❧

*M*y first Negro" is the third story in this collection to
use the Great Depression as background, but with far
varying purposes than "President Cleveland, Where Are
You?" and "Protestants Cry, too."

The mood in which I wrote "My First Negro" was both
nostalgic and rueful, and there was probably guilt mixed in
with it too. We are often prisoners of time and circumstance
and for a while in the turbulent Sixties, I felt that way. At
that time, I served as wire editor of the Fitchburg Sentinel,
which meant that I edited and wrote headlines on the
wire-service stories arriving in the newsroom on the teletype.
For a length of time, I was immersed in stories about civil
rights activities, the violent eruptions in the South; and such
names as Selma and King and Meredith became familiar
ingredients of my day as I worked to fit them into headlines
of different sizes and types. I would shoehorn words like
police dogs, fire hoses, street beatings into, say, three lines
of type confined to one column. The words became seared
into my memory.

I realized at the time how black people had played only a
small role in my life. I had grown up in a French Canadian
section of town and as a boy seldom came in contact with a
black person, or a Protestant, for that matter. In high school
and later, the few blacks I encountered seemed no different
from anyone else. The black families in town seemed to move

easily in local circles, and if there was stress or prejudice, I was unaware of it.

As the headlines accelerated, I found myself haunted by that ancient question: What if? What if racial strife came to a city much like Leominster, in the heart of New England? Could it happen? How could it happen? I began to write a novel, an act of pure imagination. In the course of writing it, I spoke at length to a black woman who had lived in the city all her life and brought up a large family. (My wife, who had been her neighbor as a child, brought us together.) The woman took me into her confidence and told me that, yes, she and her family and other blacks had encountered prejudice and bias during their lifetime, often a subtle and insidious kind of prejudice. I was appalled, and my novel began to burn within me as I wrote. The novel never found a publisher.

I also wrote a short story during that period in which I went back to my boyhood days and pondered how I might have handled a relationship with a black boy my own age. What would have happened? Would there be heroes in it or villains? Or would there be a necessity for heroes and villains?

That is what I set out to explore in "My First Negro." I wanted to capture also the essence of boyhood as I remembered it—the days of garden raids, of discovering books and that someone else loved books too. Happily, the story was published.

As to the details, there was no Alphabet Soup district in the town. Blacks were Negroes then, although some, like the fictional Jean-Paul in the story, called them "niggers." My grandfather called them "Les Noirs"—prophetic, perhaps, because noir is French for black, and years later black came into prominence.

# My First Negro 🌱

That was the summer of the long layoff at the comb shop and my father's deep silence, and Haile Selassie on the Pathe newsreel at the Globe Theater addressing the League of Nations, and Hector Langvier having a finger blown off by a homemade cherry bomb on the night before the Fourth, and the exploits of the Midnight Raiders (although we seldom stayed out later than ten o'clock or so), and, of course, Jefferson Johnson Stone. Yes, Jefferson.

As far as I was concerned, the Midnight Raiders were the most important of all. Jean-Paul LaChapelle had chosen me for two vital duties—Scout and Tomato Man. Tomatoes were highly prized—they were actually a fruit, not a vegetable at all, according to Oscar Courier, who always made the honor roll—and it was important, as you squirmed through a garden on your stomach, to be able to pick out tomatoes that were just right, not too green and not too ready for plucking but tomatoes that were on the verge of being picked by the owner in the next day or so. Jean-Paul himself was Light Man. It was his duty, shortly before the raid, to aim a rock at the nearest street light and shatter the bulb, making the area of the garden dark as midnight. Then the raiders, in the shelter of the sudden darkness, would slip and slither through the pungent rows, filling up the empty sugar sacks we had obtained at Gonthier's Meat Market.

At first, we raided the gardens for thrills, as a diversion in a summer that was somber and slumbering, and ended up gulping down the juicy tomatoes and chewing the stinging cucumbers and then having a vegetable fight, flinging the remnants at each other in desperate abandon. One evening, we saw Pamphille Rouleau passing by—he was an ancient, timid bachelor who lived alone in a small room on Third Street. As he passed, we pummeled him with our leftovers, and he danced a pathetic, pitiful jig of terror until we allowed him to scramble away. I suddenly felt sick from all I had eaten; acid burned in my chest.

"I'm getting tired of raiding gardens," Joe-Joe Toussaint said when we'd settled down in Jean-Paul's backyard to get our breaths.

I agreed with him.

Jean-Paul snapped his fingers in sudden decision. He was quick, always eager to conjure up excitement. Tall and blond and confident, he was easily our leader. Moonlight turned him silver as he asked: "Know what's the matter?"

"What?" Roger Gonthier inquired.

"We don't have a purpose," Jean-Paul said, as if reminding us of something he had repeated a million times. "We have to have a reason for raiding gardens, besides the adventure." His fingers clicked again. "I know—we'll help the poor!"

"The poor," Joe-Joe snickered.

I understood the reason for his snicker: we were all poor. Poverty had different levels, of course. There were the comfortable poor like Roger's father, who ran the market. Mr. Gonthier was a harassed, round-shouldered man hounded by something called credit. I'd heard my father say: "Poor Gonthier—he's got more credit on the books than he'll ever collect. Someday, the store's going to collapse on him." Yet, Roger and his family were always well dressed and there was dessert at every meal. Then, there were the regular poor like my own family, victims of the Depression and the seasonal tides of the comb shop. The layoffs occurred at regular times of the year, but their possible length haunted my father. That year, the summer shutdown began in June as usual, but it wore on through the Fourth of July and burned toward August. My father was always subdued during the layoffs, his huge laugh missing, and now he sank into a painful silence and stopped drinking beer as if it were Lent. We were better off, naturally, than the relief poor, families who journeyed to City Hall for small slips of paper which allowed them to stand in line and obtain plain-labeled cans and parcels of food at the commissary on Main Street. I think now that that was my father's secret dread: going on relief. At the bottom of the scale were the destitute poor, those who lived in the ramshackle buildings at the end of Frenchtown, beyond the junkyard and the city dump, in an area we called Alphabet Soup, because the streets were called simply by initials—A and B and C. The children of Alphabet Soup didn't attend St. Jude's Parochial School or even Sixth Street School, for that matter. The people there were not French or Irish or even Yankee. They seemed to be nothing: drifters, transients, rootless, and unattached.

"Alphabet Soup," Jean-Paul declared. "Tomorrow night, we raid the big Toussaint garden on Seventh Street and take the loot to Alphabet Soup. Leave it on the doorsteps there."

"Hey," Joe-Joe Toussaint said. "That's my *pépère's* garden. I can't raid my own grandfather's place."

"It's for a good cause," Jean-Paul pointed out.

"Like Robin Hood and his gang," Roger said. "Rob the rich to help the poor."

"My *pépère* isn't rich," Joe-Joe said.

As the argument wore on, I sank back into my own thoughts, dreading a Robin Hood's visit to Alphabet Soup for reasons that my friends would never guess. In fact, they would be startled to realize that, in some respects, I felt more at home there than I did in Frenchtown—and all because of Jefferson Johnson Stone. It had begun early in the summer when I had walked through the Soup, taking a shortcut from the dump, where I'd gone to collect tinfoil from empty cigarette packages along with copper wire, both of which could be sold to Jakie the Junkman, who came around every other Saturday.

"Hey, kid," a voice had called.

I turned to see a red-headed giant of a boy regarding me from twenty feet away, menace in his spread-legged stance, challenge in his yellow eyes.

My voice squeaked treacherously as I asked, "What?" I knew instantly that I was in danger.

"Come here."

I turned and ran. I arrowed between buckling buildings and shot through a slanting alleyway, my feet thudding under me and my heart throbbing inside. Behind me, I could hear the sound of my pursuer's swift feet. Looking back once to see him gaining, I pulled my ball of tinfoil from a pocket and dropped it, hoping the booty might halt his dogged chase. But he kept coming, and I knew that eventually I would be caught. Finally, as I climbed a sagging fence, hands clawed my shirt, dragging me down. I fell to the ground and looked up at him. His evil eyes smiled.

"Nutsy!"

The voice exploded like a two-inch salute in the air. My assailant hesitated.

"Nutsy, stop it."

Nutsy turned, and I followed his eyes. A figure emerged from a loose slat in a fence. I immediately thought of a Hershey bar. With almonds. He was small and thin and brown, wearing loose, lumpy, threadbare clothes. He advanced toward us, and the hostility in his manner was worse than Nutsy's potential violence. Marching with a stiff kind of dignity, he seemed to be part of an invisible parade.

"I wasn't doing anything, Jeff," Nutsy whined. "I just wanted to scare this Canuck a little."

Scowling, the newcomer waved Nutsy away with contempt. Then he directed his attention to me. I had never known a Negro, had never seen one up close, had only occasional glimpses of them uptown or in the movies— Farina in the Our Gang comedies and the perpetually frightened Negro rolling his eyes in all those Charlie Chan movies. My father referred to them as *Les Noirs*, although there were few occasions to mention Negroes. In our small New England city, they were virtually nonexistent, and in Frenchtown they were completely absent.

All of this flashed through my mind as the Negro stood over me. "What's you doing here?" he asked harshly, as Nutsy faded away.

Scrambling to my feet, I answered, "I was just taking a shortcut, and that crazy kid started chasing me."

We stared at each other. His color confounded me: I would have to tell my father that *Les Noirs* was an inaccurate description. He wasn't black at all.

I realized I owed him a debt for saving me from the young maniac with the red hair. Brushing myself off, I muttered, "Thanks."

"What did you say?" he asked, the defiance still in his

voice. Although he was possibly a year younger than I, as well as thin and scrawny, I felt that he would be a dangerous adversary.

"I said thanks." Impatience made my own voice harsh. I checked my pocket to see if my loop of copper was safe.

"What's that?" he asked.

I explained about the copper and the dump and Jakie the Junkman.

He held out his hand. I was astonished to see the pink palm, a pale island in a sea of dark flesh. Sighing, I resigned myself to the idea of highway robbery. And the wire was worth at least twenty cents.

He studied the wire for a moment or two and handed it back to me. I shoved it in my pocket, turning away, eager to leave Alphabet Soup and return to the security of my own streets.

"Know what?" he called.

"What?" I asked over my shoulder, not really interested.

"Sometimes people come down here and stare at us like we in a zoo or something," he said, the softest voice I'd ever heard, like caramel being poured lazy and sweet, skipping verbs now and then because they were too much trouble to bother with.

"You ought to get Nutsy to chase them away," I said.

"He does."

Remembering my recent close call, we both burst into laughter. To be friends, people must laugh together and later cry together, my father had often said.

"What's a Canuck?" the Negro asked, his voice suddenly childlike as he approached.

"Everybody knows what a Canuck is," I said suspiciously.

"I don't."

I explained to him about the French Canadians and how

they had left the stricken, starving farms that were drying up like puddles in the sun to seek their destinies in the glorious United States of America. Seeing his interest, I added the dubious story of how my *pépère* had sneaked one of his nephews across the border, in a sack thrown over his shoulder.

"How about you?" I asked finally.

As we walked through the neglected, debris-strewn streets, he told me that his name was Jefferson Johnson Stone, and I was awed by the splendor of the name issuing from someone so steeped in squalor. With a name like that, he should own the world and stride the streets like a king.

Remembering the history books in school, I longed to ask if his people had been slaves. But I didn't want to insult him.

"Do you come from the South?" I hazarded.

He explained that his family came from a place outside of Boston. His father was looking for work. Jefferson had four brothers and three sisters. I was disappointed by his matter-of-fact recital; it sounded like the story of a regular Canuck family.

He pointed out his house, a small dilapidated structure, gaunt and weary, clothes hanging like flags of surrender on sagging lines. The odor of something fried a long time ago stained the air.

"We only been here a few weeks," Jefferson said. "My ma's still scrubbing the inside to make it homelike."

Still trying to salvage drama, I summoned countless questions. For instance, I'd read in school about the Underground Railroad that had brought slaves to freedom in the North around Civil War times. Was that how Jefferson's family had gotten to Boston?

"You like bread and sugar?" Jefferson asked, as we made our way toward the back steps of his house.

I nodded, although I'd never heard of that particular combination before. However, in those days, my stomach welcomed anything edible.

His mother was washing clothes in a bucket in the backyard while his father chopped wood. Children were scattered here and there, brown and tight-haired and big-eyed. No one paid any attention to me. The scent of spices emanated from the kitchen, destroying the stale, fried smell that hovered in the air outside. Jefferson took rough slices of bread from an oil-cloth-covered box on the kitchen shelf and passed them under the trickly faucet. He sprinkled sugar on the damp surface of the bread.

"This week everybody got extra sugar at the commissary," he said. "Surplus, they call it. My dad's too proud to go—but I don't mind."

This attitude surprised me, because Jefferson carried himself like the proudest person I'd ever seen. I followed him through the doorway into the living room and was pondering with curiosity a plush velvet davenport that stood beside a brass bed—when I saw the pile of books on a table.

"That red sofa," Jefferson was saying, "Ma said she could never leave it behind in Boston, so we took it with us. Pa bought it for her on their honeymoon."

But I was scrutinizing the book titles: *The Sea Wolf*, by Jack London, *Sonnets from the Portuguese*, *The Complete Poems of Robert W. Service*, Zane Grey's *Riders of the Purple Sage*.

"These your books?" I asked.

His eyes slid away from me, and his hands seemed to be flying everywhere. I realized he was embarrassed.

Partly to allay his embarrassment and partly out of a

leaping gladness, I said: "You like Robert W. Service? Wow! And Jack London! Did you read *Call of the Wild?*" I didn't dare mention the sonnets—"How do I love thee? Let me count the ways"—because I myself would have blushed. Yet, the sonnets had assuaged my aching spirit the spring before, when I fell hopelessly in love with Yvonne Blanchemaison.

The books launched us on a long conversation as we ate the limp bread, food that I didn't find to my taste but that I swallowed out of politeness. But it was the good, rich talk that counted. Outside, in the shade of a weeping willow tree, we discussed our favorite authors, and I was astounded to discover that there was another fellow my age who sometimes liked a book more than a ball game.

Thus began my friendship with Jefferson Johnson Stone, although I didn't regard it as friendship at the time. Brought together by books, we soon branched out and found other mutual interests. Collecting rocks, some of which looked like ancient Indian arrowheads. Practicing the quick draw with toy pistols. But mostly, it was the books. And music. He told me that one of his uncles was a jazz musician in Boston.

Jefferson didn't have a library card, because he wasn't yet enrolled in school, so I checked out books on my own card and brought them to him. I asked him to meet me at the library, where we might explore the stacks together, but he always found some excuse for not coming. I didn't press the issue, just as I preferred to visit him in Alphabet Soup rather than meet him somewhere in Frenchtown. I didn't think twice about these circumstances; they just seemed natural. Somehow, Jefferson seemed to belong to the Soup. I couldn't picture him away from there.

All during that summer, I journeyed to his neighborhood

two or three times a week, always carrying a book or two. Once I brought my stamp collection, and another time my book of Frenchtown statistics. In those days, I was a great collector of data, passing the time by counting, for instance, the number of street lights lining Mechanic Street, how many elm trees grew on Third Street, how many three-story tenement houses there were in Frenchtown (I'd covered the first six streets at that time).

I was also secretive and felt a need for privacy. Just as my notebooks were a secret shared only with Jefferson, so were my visits to Alphabet Soup. I would steal away from Third Street, headed for a meeting with Jefferson, and the fact that no one knew my destination added drama to my visits. When Roger Gonthier asked me once where I disappeared to all the time, I smiled mysteriously. Afraid that he might follow me and regarding the threat as constituting a contest of skills, I always took a circuitous route to the Soup. It was almost like the movies.

After that first meeting when we had talked about our families, we ignored our backgrounds and asked no more questions. The fact that he was a Negro occurred only once in conversation. Nutsy came walking toward us one afternoon and gave us wide berth when we passed, looking at Jefferson in obvious terror.

Jefferson chuckled, a dry sound. I realized he didn't smile very often.

"That Nutsy," he said. "He's afraid of me."

"Why?" Nutsy was almost a head taller and perhaps thirty pounds heavier.

"He thinks I'm the bogeyman," Jefferson said. "Lots of people think that way. Pa says, 'We in the Soup, all right.' He wants to go back to Boston. Live with our own kind. No work here, and everybody lonesome." He kicked at a stone, that odd embarrassment deepening his skin again. "I ain't too lonesome."

I myself blushed, flattered that perhaps our friendship had helped him conquer the loneliness. Thinking of the Midnight Raiders, I wondered whether it might be possible for Jefferson to become a member. His dark skin would give him a natural protection, and his thin, wiry body would make him an excellent squirmer through narrow garden rows. But I thought of all the complications, vague as they were in my mind, and dismissed it.

In an attempt to sympathize with him, I said, "My father's out of work, too."

"Yeah," said Jefferson. "But he's got a job to be *out* of. My pa's got nothin' at all." Again, that syrup covered his words, but this time there was a bitterness in it. I felt as though he were rebuking me.

Silence fell between us, but not the companionable silence we had shared earlier. The afternoon seemed unbearably hot, all of a sudden, too hot to do anything. Finally, I made some sort of excuse and left. And it was the night of that same day that I sprawled on the ground listening to Jean-Paul outline plans for raiding the Toussaint garden and taking the vegetables to Alphabet Soup.

"Can't we take the stuff someplace else?" Roger Gonthier asked.

"You afraid?" Jean-Paul challenged.

"Yes," Roger admitted. As we all knew, Roger wasn't the bravest fellow in the world, but he was honest.

"Listen, that's where the real poor people live," Jean-Paul said. "There's even some niggers there."

"Negroes," I corrected.

Jean-Paul looked at me, puzzled. "That's what I said. There's a family of niggers there."

I realized he had made no distinction between the words, and I was troubled for some reason.

"My *pépère's* garden is a tough one," Joe-Joe said, still doubtful about the ethics of stealing from his own grandfather.

"A garden is a garden," Jean-Paul pronounced. "We have our Scout and we have a Light Man." He and I exchanged looks of pride.

"You'll need more than just one Light Man," Joe-Joe countered. "My *pépère's* got a light on the back piazza—and it stays on until he goes to bed. About midnight."

I thought of Jefferson and what a Raider he would have made, his dark skin blending with the shadows. In sudden inspiration, I blurted out, "Hey, why don't we put black stuff on our faces?"

"With cork," Jean-Paul said, slapping his hands together.

"Stove black," Oscar Courier suggested.

And immediately I was sorry for having made the suggestion, as if I were insulting Jefferson in some manner. In fact, I was doubtful about the entire Alphabet Soup plan.

"A terrific idea," Jean-Paul said, slapping me on the shoulder. He plunged into details: obtaining corks from the wine bottles in his uncle's cellar and inspecting the Soup to see which families were most deserving. I was thankful that he did not assign me to scout Alphabet Soup.

The raid on the Toussaint garden, two nights later, was a thing of beauty. With burnt cork smeared on our hands and faces and wearing our darkest clothes, we didn't bother knocking out any lights at all. Roger's grandfather was such a suspicious type that a shattered light bulb would merely put him on his guard. The garden was at its height of ripeness, lush with tomatoes and cucumbers and all the other vegetables. Our sugar bags were quickly filled. Then we stole through the streets of Frenchtown, black-faced ghosts, laden with our treasures. A barking dog greeted us at the edge of Alphabet Soup, but Roger Gonthier quieted him immediately. It was later than usual. Because we had raided the garden in the glare of street lights and in the glow of a full moon, we'd waited until after ten o'clock for the attack. Passersby were as much a danger as garden owners.

Jean-Paul halted us. "Here we are."

We crouched near some bushes by an abandoned shack. Jefferson's house was across the street, a dim light shining in a front room. Music emanating from a tinny phonograph floated in the air. I felt vulnerable suddenly, as if on a brightly lit stage.

"Let's get going," I urged, wanting to be done with it.

Now we stole across the street, each assigned a particular house in the neighborhood. To my relief, I had not been chosen to leave my vegetables at Jefferson's.

"Who's that?" a voice called sharply.

We froze in our tracks, a frightened tableau.

A flashlight stabbed the air, its ray a long, bright dagger.

Another shout. A lantern leaped to life on Jefferson's porch.

"What do we do?" Joe-Joe whispered frantically.

Never had the moonlight seemed so bright as we crouched there in the gutter.

Before Jean-Paul could answer, a rock sailed through the air. I saw it skimming toward us but was powerless to intercept it or even shout a warning. It struck Roger Gonthier on the cheek, and he bellowed with pain. Always swift to react, Jean-Paul dug into his bag of vegetables.

"Let them have it," he commanded, flinging a cucumber

in the general direction of Jefferson's house, where all the lights now blazed with brilliance. People were rushing around wildly in the front yard.

We threw a barrage of vegetables in all directions, hurling them blindly as fast as we could pick them, pulled back our arms, and let them fly through the air. At the same time, we slowly retreated down the street. Islands of illumination flickered and flared as more lanterns and flashlights were brought out. We seemed to have the advantage for the moment; our artillery was immediately at hand, and we didn't have to grope around for stones. Once in a while, we heard the satisfying squish of a tomato hitting a target. Dogs barked, children screamed.

"We're under attack," someone cried.

A window shattered.

"Let's get out of here," Jean-Paul yelled, dropping his bag as we neared the end of the street.

I aimed my last tomato and began to gallop after the others, hearing the sounds of pursuit. A few more steps and I would be out of danger, because there was an area between Alphabet Soup and Frenchtown where there were no street lights and darkness would offer protection. Trailing my companions, I turned on my speed, despite the burning in my lungs. Footsteps drew dangerously close behind me. Suddenly, I tripped and pitched headlong to the gravel. A body flung itself upon me, and I twisted around to defend myself.

I found myself staring into the eyes of Jefferson Johnson Stone.

Those eyes. Stunned with surprise, as if a twig had snapped across them. Wide with disbelief. And a terrible bewilderment, such a bewilderment that he loosened his grip, and I took advantage of it to pull myself away and leap to my feet. My face was stiff with the burnt cork, and my arm ached where I had fallen upon it. Footsteps pounded around us as other people from the Soup carried on the chase. I wanted to say something to him—but what? And I was still in danger; I had to get out of there. So I turned and ran, tears spilling down my cheeks and my arm throbbing. I didn't look behind.

The weather broke in in the next few days, the dry, dusty heat washed away by rainstorms—heavy, stay-in-the-house kind of rain, rain to read the latest Penrod and Sam by. But I was restless and uninterested. Even the arrival of the new Ken Maynard movie at the Globe failed to arouse my enthusiasm, although I spent my last ten cents to attend.

I arrived home late in the afternoon in the melancholy of a gray, sad rain, to see a scarlet patch flung across our back door; someone had thrown tomatoes at the door, and the juice ran down the wood like blood from a wound. I found a rag and filled a basin with water and began to wash off the scarlet stains. My mother sputtered, watching me, indignant at what the world was coming to.

"Who would do such a crazy thing?" she asked. I didn't say anything.

A few days later, I journeyed again to Alphabet Soup. The rain had ceased and the storm clouds had moved off, taking summer with them. Most of the gardens sagged dismally, tomato poles leaning wearily, some having toppled to the ground from the force of the rain. My footsteps lagged; I was reluctant to face Jefferson. Would I be able to explain to him? About the face I wore that night? My failure—not bringing him to Frenchtown? A thousand things?

Finally, I arrived at the Soup and stared unbelievingly at Jefferson's house. The place was deserted, the house wearing the unmistakable look of vacancy.

"They're gone."

I turned to see Nutsy calling from across the street.

"Where?"

"Back to Boston," Nutsy said.

I thought of Jefferson's eyes, eyes that could flash with anger, eyes that could blaze with hate. Proud Jefferson. I thought of the dignity he wore like a suit of armor. And those tomatoes hurled at my back door.

I knew that somewhere in Boston, somewhere in the big world outside of Alphabet Soup and Frenchtown, I had an enemy, an enemy for life, waiting, waiting.

"Hey, Canuck. You one of them that attacked us with the tomatoes? All blacked up like niggers?"

A denial sprang to my lips, but I didn't say anything.

"You don't look so tough without Jeff around," Nutsy said, advancing, his eyes still yellow.

But I didn't run.

My chin trembled and tears welled in my eyes, and I thought *Oh Jefferson, Oh Jefferson*, and I knew that Nutsy was bigger and a better fighter, but I stood there anyway, waiting for him to cross the street.

# Bunny Berigan—
## Wasn't He a
## Musician or
## Something?

# Introduction 🌿

"**B**unny Berigan—Wasn't He a Musician or Something?" is in sharp contrast to the other stories in this collection. There's not a child or a teenager—or a wife—in sight.

Why include it then? Because wives and children are very much presences in this story. Although they don't appear physically, they haunt almost every paragraph and lurk between the lines.

For those reasons, the story is included here in addition to the first eight—the discordant note that perhaps deepens the sound of the others.

There's also another reason.

The story is a particular favorite of mine because it emerged on paper exactly as I envisioned it. Which does not always happen, of course. Ordinarily, readers don't see how far short the writer falls of his goal, how impoverished the actual story is to the original concept. Readers see only the finished product; they haven't seen the stumbling starts, the waste-basket pages, the metaphors that went askew, the stillborn phrases.

The concept of this story came to me in a flash. I saw it all in my mind, like scenes from a passing train—the characters, the events, the tone, the second level. But it wasn't written in a flash. The story was written painstakingly, sentence by sentence, but with tenderness and care and with *the certainty that the material was under control, the characters behaving the way they should, the mood sustained until the final word.*

*I can't imagine a collection of my stories without this one.*

# Bunny Berigan— Wasn't He a Musician or Something? 🌿

One thing I'll say about him. He didn't stall, he didn't beat around the bush or try to justify himself with excuses and alibis. He didn't even wait for the martinis to be served. As soon as the order was given he said, "I asked Ellen for a divorce last night."

I had heard rumors about Walt and some girl, and so I wasn't completely surprised, although I had discounted the whispers at the time. Walt Crane and another woman? Ridiculous. Maybe a cocktail once in a while, but not in some secluded rendezvous. And maybe some flirting in a half-joking way, because I had heard that the girl was a knockout, a model, and she and Walt were thrown together occasionally at the advertising agency where he worked. But it would have been nothing more than that because these things didn't happen to people like Walt and me. We weren't kids any more; we had children almost grown up. We took naps after supper and were slightly overweight. We were getting nostalgic and sentimental, beginning sentences with words like "I remember when I was a boy" while the kids looked skyward in thinly disguised impatience. Walt and I were old friends who had been through school and a war together, and we didn't get divorces from our wives. Until now.

"What happened, Walt?" I asked, stalling for time. "Last I heard, you and Ellen were thinking of buying a new car, and little Sandra had the measles, Tommy had got a lousy report card and Debbie was walking on air because she was going to her first formal. And now, all of a sudden, a divorce?"

He grimaced as if absorbing pain, and looked up gratefully as the waiter returned with our drinks. I watched him sipping the drink and figured that it probably did some good to have me conjure up a picture of his home and kids and Ellen, who was lovely and tender even though she possessed a quick temper that exploded over small annoyances and sent her into the prison of migraines.

He put down the glass and raised his hands, palms upward, in resignation. "I know what you're thinking, Jerry. That I'm the villain of the thing. Fine, I admit it. But it's never quite that simple."

Oh, hell, I thought, who am I to act as judge and jury? Yet I thought of Ellen—"poor Ellen," people would be saying now—and I looked around for a weapon.

"How did Ellen take the news?" I asked, knowing, of course, that he didn't want to discuss her at all. And I knew I had found my weapon.

He frowned, shaking his head, avoiding my eyes. "Hard, Jerry, she took it hard. She didn't have an inkling; she hadn't suspected a thing. Oh, she knew I'd been acting different lately. But she thought I was worried about the job, working too hard on the new presentations." His words came out helter-skelter, falling on top of each other, and I was surprised at the genuine pain in them.

"Anyway, I think she's numb right now. She cried and my heart broke for her, but there was nothing I could do, Jerry. I had to tell her. I had to make the break . . ."

"Is it the model?" I asked.

"You've heard about her?"

"Rumors. Vague stuff. I figured it was just a lot of talk."

"You figured it wasn't possible, right?" he asked laconically. "Not good old Walter Crane. Old faithful. Captain of the bowling team at the office. Past treasurer of the PTA. But it happens, Jerry, to people like me. To people like you and me. We don't go looking for it, but it happens. Or change that—maybe we are looking for it, maybe everybody is, but we don't like to admit it . . ."

His accusation wasn't sharp enough to cause me any pangs of conscience. I was safe, sitting across from him, thinking about the bonus that was scheduled later in the month at the office, wondering whether my latest sales figures would break a record for October, remembering suddenly the birthday party that night for Kathy, my teenaged daughter, who lived in a world of either brilliant laughter or desperate tears. And hadn't Harriet asked me to bring home two gallons (*two* gallons?) of ice cream this afternoon?

"Ah, Jerry," he was saying, his fingers steepled, his voice hushed as if he were in church, "she's terrific. Wonderful. Her name is Jennifer West and she's so beautiful it hurts." He shook his head, his eyes reaching for distances, a poet trying to pin down the one word that would describe it all.

"How did all this happen?" I asked wearily. I didn't really want to hear the details—how they had met, who had introduced them, the tentative advance, the first drink together, the looking deep into each other's eyes, the first caress. He did not have to spell out those details because everyone has read or heard about those things a million times or more, and it is not new or exciting or meaningful except to the newest lovers who are discovering it all over again. And I was reluctant to have Walt recount the details because I had become too accustomed to him in another role—delicately pulling a splinter from little Tommy's finger that time we all went on a fishing trip to Maine, or splashing Debbie mercilessly at the beach on the Cape to get her mind off her broken heart, or sitting on the sagging porch of a rented cottage after a day of sunshine and water, the kids sleeping inside, he and Ellen and Harriet and I sipping beer quietly, agreeing in one of those sudden profound moments of contentment that life was good, life was kind . . . I had seen him too often in the role of husband and father, and that was why I was reluctant now to hear him speak of a love affair that had nothing to do with splinters and splashing daughters.

"At first I thought it was ridiculous, Jerry," he was saying, "that this girl could care for me, could see anything in me. I mean, here I am, an old married man, all settled down. And there she was, young, beautiful, and maybe a thousand guys waiting for her to give them a tumble . . ."

Again he shook his head at the wonder of it all. "Anyway, it happened accidentally. The heel came off her shoe as she walked into my office, and I was coming around the corner, and . . ."

"Like in the movies," I said.

His lips pressed themselves into a grimace, and I could have sworn that I saw some terrible sadness cross his features, a sadness that had nothing to do with my gibe. Somehow he suddenly seemed vulnerable.

"Go ahead," I said, softening the edge in my voice. "Tell me the rest."

"There isn't much to tell, Jerry," he said, the eagerness returning, the sadness gone as swiftly as it had appeared, "because a lot of stuff you can't put into words. Do you think I'm kidding myself? I know what you're thinking, and it's the same thing I'd be thinking if the shoe were on the other foot—that I'm a damned fool, that I'm throwing myself away, my whole life away, on a girl who . . ."

I realized then that my role of antagonist was ridiculous, that it would gain neither of us anything.

"Getting back to Ellen," I said. "Did she agree to let you go?"

"I think she will eventually. She was too upset last night to settle anything. But she knows that I'm not just talking. I packed my clothes . . ."

"Where are you living?"

"In Jennifer's apartment building," he said. Then he held up his hand as if halting traffic. "But not in her apartment. Upstairs, directly over her place." He had a look of self-righteousness on his face.

"Did you make any arrangements with Ellen?" I asked. "I mean finances, things like that. It's going to be tough, Walt, juggling two households."

He signaled for two more martinis, and the waiter caught his eye immediately. Previously he had resembled me— unable to capture a waiter's attention, standing in the line that didn't move at the bank, betting on the wrong ball team. Now, seeing his instant success with the waiter, I wondered if he had become endowed with a new quality, if the girl had brought him a certain assurance and an aura of success.

We were silent while the waiter served the second round. After his departure, Walt leaned forward, his knuckles white where he gripped the stem of the glass. "Jerry, Jerry," he said, his voice oddly pained. "Don't you think I've been through all this? You talk about finances, money . . . that's only a small part of it, the smallest part. Jennifer earns enough to make up the difference so that I can take good care of Ellen and the kids. They'll have nothing to worry about on that score. But it's the other things . . ." He sipped the martini, looking away from me. "Like kissing the kids goodbye last night. They didn't know I was kissing them goodbye, of course. Ellen was in the living room, huddled up, crying quietly, trying not to make a scene. Good old Ellen. And I went upstairs and looked in on the girls. They looked so innocent, as if they had no defenses against the world. I kissed them in their sleep, and I never loved them as much as at that moment. And then I felt sadness come over me, because I knew that I was committing myself. Up until that time I'd been carrying on an affair with Jennifer, and it all had been wild and wonderful in spite of knowing that I was the biggest heel in the world behind Ellen's back. But it was still terrific, like being drunk on champagne and never getting a hangover. There in the bedroom with the girls, though, I realized that by telling Ellen, I'd committed myself, I'd burned my bridges . . ." His voice faltered.

"Anyway," he continued, "that was the moment of truth, in the bedroom with the girls, kissing them on the cheek, and touching Sandra's bruises—she fell off her bike the day before and hurt her chin—that was when I knew there was no turning back . . ."

"Did you want to turn back?" I asked gently, sensing the agony of his moment in the bedroom. "I mean, for one moment there did you wish that it hadn't happened, that you hadn't met her?"

He was silent for a moment or two, and when he spoke his voice came out almost in a whisper.

"I didn't go that far, Jerry. I couldn't. I'd already told Ellen, and I'd known from the start that it would hurt, that we'd all be hurt in some way. Jerry, it's easy for you to sit there judging me, thinking that I'm different, that I don't feel things the way other people do and that that's why I was able to walk out on my wife and kids last night. But that isn't the way it is, not at all. I didn't all of a sudden turn into somebody else. I'm still Walt Crane. I still love my kids." He pushed the glass away. "Look, by the time I got to Tommy's room last night I was wrung out. The girls were bad enough, but Tommy . . . well, I'd seen myself in him so many times. That's what really hurt, kissing him good-night, goodbye, knowing that when he woke up the world would be changed for him."

"But you did it, Walt. All that didn't stop you," I said, trying to understand what kind of love could make a fellow take a step like this, planning a life with his children left out of it.

"That's right, I did it," he said. "But Jennifer's worth it all. It's like"—he groped for the word—"like being born again."

I thought: He'll be quoting poetry next.

"So there it is, Jerry. I wanted to tell you myself, before you heard it from somebody else."

"Well, I appreciate that, Walt. We've been through a lot together, the good times and the bad."

"And I want you to meet her, Jerry," he said.

"Fine, Walt, fine," I replied automatically, preparing to pay the check, knowing that the conversation was over, that a certain way of life was over.

"She's supposed to meet us here," he said. "She should be here any minute."

His words did not carry their meaning to me immediately because I was thinking of that bedroom where Walt had kissed his daughters goodbye while they lay sleeping, thinking that their world was still bright and safe and secure. I thought of my own children, Kathy and Joey and little

Carol, and how much I loved them. But I knew that I didn't love them any more than Walt loved his. And through the sadness that accompanied these thoughts I realized what Walt had said.

"She's coming here? To meet us?" I asked.

"I want you to know her, Jerry, to find out how wonderful she is," Walt explained. "I know what everyone thinks of someone like Jennifer. What do they call her—the other woman, the homewrecker? All those clichés. But when you see her face to face, you'll know what I mean . . ."

He looked beyond my shoulder toward the door, and I saw the flashing in his eyes, the youth that suddenly raced across his features like a sunrise, the way he half-raised himself from his chair—I knew that Jennifer West had entered the place and drawn him to her like a magnet.

She was heart-wrenchingly beautiful. A brunette, with violets for eyes, pale skin, young. So young, achingly young. Walt seemed to be drinking in her loveliness as she approached, forgetting me, forgetting the bar's clatter and everything else as he looked at her. My own eyes were on her. Old Walt, with a girl like that to love.

He stumbled through the introductions as he went around the table and pulled out a chair for her. "My best friend," he said, nodding toward me. And inclining his head toward her, he said to me, "My best girl."

If she hadn't been so beautiful and if he hadn't looked so happy, the little introductions would have seemed ludicrous. Jennifer West acknowledged her introduction with a radiant smile that revealed perfect teeth and a sudden dimple in her cheek. I could see the thing she had in her smile—she could look at one person as if there were nobody else alive in the world. She looked at me that way for a moment, and when she turned away there was a sense of loss because I knew she looked at other people in that manner for only an instant or two, while she gazed at Walt continually that way. But before she turned away, she said, "I'm glad to meet you, Mr.—"

"Please call me Jerry."

"—Jerry, because Walt's spoken so much about you that I feel we've known each other for a long time."

Where do I go from here? I asked myself. Stay or leave? I didn't want to betray Ellen and the old life that all of us—Walt and Ellen, Harriet and I and the children—had shared, by sitting there pretending to condone what Walt was doing, by pretending that this girl Jennifer West was a welcome arrival. But I have always been a coward in small gestures, betraying myself in a million ways—laughing at a dirty joke that isn't really funny, remaining silent when someone makes a nasty crack about somebody who's left the room, never wanting to make a fuss, avoiding embarrassing situations. And so I decided to paste a polite smile on my face and stick it out awhile, noncommittal, until I could leave after a decent interval.

Jennifer West disarmed me by saying, "I'm sorry to make you so uncomfortable, Jerry, but please don't blame me. Walt insisted that I meet you, even though I told him from the beginning that you had every right to resent me."

She was probably twenty-two years old, but she spoke and held herself with a dignity beyond her years. Her poise perhaps stemmed from her training as a model, although I felt that she had been born with that regal manner. I could see why Walt did not speak of her as "Jenny" or "Jen," but referred to her always as "Jennifer." When she was seven years old and little boys in the second grade were fighting over her at recess, she'd probably been called Jennifer. And she must have had that warmth, that intimacy, in her eyes even then.

I remembered suddenly that she had addressed me directly, something about resenting her.

"Look, Jennifer, I'm not a judge or jury," I said, knowing the contempt I would fling at myself later for not taking a stand here and now, for not showing how I really felt about it all. "Walt's not a kid any more . . ."

She reached out and closed her hand over his, a small act of defiance—more than defiance, possession. And I felt left out, as if I were sitting at another table.

The waiter hovered nearby, awaiting her order. "Martinis all around," Walt said.

"He's corrupting me," she said to me. "My speed used to be weak daiquiris."

Speaking of corruption, I should have said, you haven't done too badly with him, either. But I didn't, of course. Instead I said, "Do you like modeling?" and listened intently to her answer, noticing the small, lovely hint of down on one ear, and her eyes which, incredibly, changed color as you looked at them, violet to gray and back again. The third martini is always the one that softens the edges of everything, and it tasted wonderfully dry and stinging; the jukebox, or whatever they had in the bar, played softly in the background, some old song I couldn't quite remember but that reminded me of dances after football games at school. As we sat there I studied her surreptitiously, including Walt in my scrutiny. He still wore a crew cut, but when he inclined his head the pink scalp was visible through the thinning hair. His face had been slashed by time, the erosions of the years. Jennifer's skin was without blemish, her ebony hair was luxuriant, her eyes were sparkling. They seemed an unlikely couple, certainly, the young and the old. But Walt's evidence of age didn't seem to matter. He sat alertly beside her, like a small boy preening, immersed in her words, basking in her presence, responding to every nuance of her tone or gesture. Once in a while he'd look at me, pride stamped on his face, as if to say, What do you think of her, Jerry? Isn't she worth it all? And I would smile at him, a small, stingy smile that hid what I really was beginning to think: that she was one of the loveliest girls I'd ever seen, so lovely that it caused a pain in my chest.

"I want to know everything about Walt," she was saying. "Tell me about him, Jerry, all the things he likes and dislikes, so that I can make him happy."

"Well, let me see, now," I said, falling in with the game, carried on the waves of the third martini and feeling a warmth for Walt, my old buddy. "He's not really a martini man but a beer drinker. Don't ask him about his war experiences, because he tries to look modest but finally he'll tell you how he lost his Good Conduct Medal in a barroom in Naples on a wild weekend. He'll tell you that he can't stand television, but he sits up till two o'clock watching 'The Late Late Show.'"

My words sounded cleverer than they really were, and Jennifer was caught up in them because of her love for Walt; and Walt pretended embarrassment but seemed actually to be enjoying himself.

"And, let's see," I continued, sipping the drink, savoring the taste, "He likes Hemingway and Steinbeck who wrote *The Grapes of Wrath*, and Brubeck and Ellington. And his prized possession is an original recording of 'I Can't Get Started' by Bunny Berigan."

A frown scrawled itself across her forehead. "Wait a minute," she said. "You're getting ahead of me. Bunny

Berigan?" The dimple asserted itself as she wrinkled her nose in concentration. "Bunny Berigan," she mused, turning to Walt. "Wasn't he a musician or something?"

"That's right," he said. "He played a great trumpet, and that song Jerry mentioned, 'I Can't Get Started,' broke all our hearts back in those days." He closed his eyes for a moment, as if he could hear that tortured horn reaching for the high one even now. And those old echoes, if that is what he could hear, brought a sadness to his face.

"Well," she said, briskly businesslike, "I'll have to add Bunny Berigan to my list of things to catch up on."

Walt looked at me, pride in his eyes. "She learns fast," he said, but I still detected the sadness there. I wondered if he was hearing somehow, that sorrowful song that poor tragic Bunny Berigan had played so long ago. Or was there another reason?

"Jennifer," I said, a small excitement in my voice, "ever hear of bank night?"

She shook her head.

"*Winterset?* With Burgess Meredith as Mio?"

She regarded me blankly.

"A song called 'Rosalie'?"

Still nothing.

"Baby-Face Nelson? Fireside Chats? Gas rationing? The sit-down strikes? 'Pete Smith Specialties'? 'One for the Gipper'?"

She looked at me as if I had lost my senses, as if I had begun to speak some strange, unknown language, and she turned to Walt in an appeal for assistance, rescue. But he wasn't, for once, looking at her. He was studying me, his face naked and unguarded, caught in some loneliness, a loneliness I had mistaken simply for pain earlier in our conversation.

"How do you feel about naps after supper?" I asked her.

She smiled, a patient answer, having decided that the martinis had reached me.

"I've got to rush off to a fitting, honey," she told Walt. Turning to me, laughing softly, she said, "Jerry, it was so nice meeting you. You've got to tell me all about those— what did you call them?—'Pete Smith Specialties' sometime."

Walt scraped his chair as he rose. "Yes, we'll have to get together soon," he said hurriedly. "I'll give you a ring, Jerry." He seemed on edge, trying to smooth out our goodbye and signaling the waiter for the check and fumbling for his wallet and wanting to leave with Jennifer, naturally. What man wouldn't want to walk out of a bar with a lovely thing like Jennifer West on his arm? He scurried in Jennifer's wake while I lighted another cigarette and thought, What will you do, Walt, when the bloom leaves Jennifer, as it left Ellen and leaves everybody?

I guided myself through the revolving doors and emerged into the afternoon sun, dazzled by the onslaught of light, the way it used to be on Saturday afternoons when I'd come out of the Globe Theater into the real world, vivid and eye-shattering, after the black-and-white exploits of Tim McCoy or Hoot Gibson.

Hey, Jennifer, ever hear of Hoot Gibson?

I signaled for a passing cab, suddenly realizing that I was overdue at the office. As the car drew up, a girl stepped smartly into my range of vision. She wore a crazy candy-striped beret and had blond bangs. She looked at me charmingly, coquettishly, but she still beat me to the cab.

The taxi took her away and left me standing there on the sidewalk, thinking of Walt, poor Walt, and Jennifer, who had never heard of Fireside Chats or sit-down strikes, as lovely as she was. I watched the taxi bearing away the beautiful girl wearing the crazy beret and thought: How lucky some of us are! Lucky, because we have the temptations but not the opportunities, because we're always missing the cabs or the elevators or the trains that might have changed our lives and that would lead us eventually to the hell that always awaits the ones who break the rules. Like Walt. And I wondered—if I was so happy to have missed that possible hell—why I felt like crying, standing on the sidewalk, surrounded by people, at two-thirty in the afternoon.

# Robert Cormier

*whose stunning and superbly crafted novels have won the highest critical acclaim, began his career as a newspaperman over twenty-five years ago. He has been involved in all phases of journalism, has twice received the Associated Press award for the Best News Story in New England, and is now devoting his full time to writing. Mr. Cormier is the author of six novels, including the award-winning* The Chocolate War *and* I Am the Cheese, *and most recently,* After the First Death, *which was selected by the American Library Association as one of the Best Books for Young Adults of 1979.*